IN TOO DEEP

THE MURDER OF BUSTER CRABB

JAN NEEDLE

© Jan Needle 2016

Jan Needle has asserted his rights under the Copyright, Design and Patents Act, 1988, to be identified as the author of this work.

First published in 2016 by Endeavour Press

For Tim, Sue, and all the other Beatties

Thanks for everything

Historical Note

Lionel 'Buster' Crabb was a frogman sent by MI6 – strictly against the orders of the Government – to undertake a top secret mission against a Soviet cruiser bringing two of Russia's most important leaders, Nikita Khrushchev and Nikolai Bulganin, on a 'courtesy visit' to England to ease the growing tensions between the East and West. What exactly happened in the murky depths of Portsmouth Harbour has been declared a secret of the State, bizarrely, for another 40 years.

It was 1956, with the Cold War at a critically fissile stage, but men like Ian Fleming, the naval spy who created 007, and Nicholas Elliott, head of the SIS London Station, were much more gung-ho than their elected masters. Stalwarts of the 'Eton mafia' – rich, young and bursting with self-confidence – they called themselves the Robber Barons.

Unlike Prime Minister Sir Anthony Eden, who had personally forbidden such an expedition, they were sure their plan was brilliant – and fool-proof. They were invincible.

And Buster Crabb was never seen alive again.

One

He was having that dream again. He lay beside her in her comfortable, pristine double bed, and by now it was more like a battlefield. He was a small man, but strong and wiry, and for minutes he had been twisting and writhing like a thing possessed by demons. Pat, as so many times before, did not know what to do.

If she woke him, anything could happen. Once, he had stared at her with eyes filled with rage and hatred, then had thrown himself across the bed at her, one fist drawn back to smash her in the face. She had tried to find it funny that his misjudged momentum had shot him straight off the other side to crash down to the floor. She had failed.

The most frustrating thing was that he would never tell her what the dream was about. She knew it was the same one every time, because some of the words he mumbled or shouted never changed. He was underwater, with a knife, and someone was going to kill him.

Pat Rose had been with him for years now, on and off, and her love was mixed with fear and pity.

He would talk about the war in general terms to her, but never on specifics. She had read about him in the papers, though, and in the bar in Chatham where they'd met he was reckoned as a sort of giant. Which considering his stature, struck Pat as endearing; and quite sweet.

He had never claimed himself, even the first time they'd gone to bed together, to be a hero. When she had suggested it, in fact, he'd blushed just like a baby. But he had the George Medal, he admitted, and 'a couple of other stupid gongs' besides. He'd made a croaking noise.

'I'm a frog,' he said. 'That's why I walk so bloody funny.'

'And I'm a barmaid,' Pat returned. 'Ruddy hell, love! You could do better than a skivvy if you wanted to!'

But that, apparently, he could not understand. At first she thought he was putting it on, but he convinced her.

'What you talking about, gal? What's it matter what you work as? Bleeding hell, don't talk so fucking stupid.'

Instead of picking him up on his language, Pat Rose fell in love. She made a noise, Lionel misinterpreted it and apologised for his swearing, and they ended up in a sexy heap. It was the nicest pickup night she could remember. That either of them could, in fact. And in the first flush of excitement, maybe, he had had no violent dreams.

That had been in Chatham, though, and they lived in London now. Truth is, that was where she'd followed him to, left her home and friends and family. She'd hoped for marriage, and after a while expected it would happen. He was a good man. Kind and generous, and very, very funny.

And he wasn't a wanderer, despite what her girlfriends told her. He was something in the Navy, and of course he had to go off to other places to do work from time to time. Work was like the dreams, though: he wouldn't say exactly what he did. A diver, yeah, a frogman, but so what? The war was over. It was the Fifties. They didn't have an enemy any more.

But he did have secrets, and Pat learned them bitterly. That he drank too much, that he went off with dirty women from time to time, and finally, that he was even married. That had been the bitterest. And wife Margaret was a barmaid too, just like her. Except that she claimed something different now, as did Pat. Pat was a typist by this time, a secretary, she earned a decent wage. She could do ninety words a minute Pitmans.

'And what does she do now?' she screamed, when he admitted that the rumour was correct. 'You bastard, Lionel, you rotten, rotten bastard! I s'pose she's a better class than me, is she? I bet she... I bet she...'

Disarmingly, he'd laughed.

'A better class of barmaid, or a secretary?' he said. 'I 'spect she even gets to put the pencils out!'

Her lips were shaking, and he took her in his arms and embraced her, hard. He was strong, she'd always loved it. And then he coughed, and she coughed, and they shared another fag. His marriage had lasted seven months, he said. It had been another of his big mistakes. A bigger one than usual.

'Like me,' she said. 'Like me, Lionel. Like bloody me!'

'I do like you,' he said. 'Despite your bloody language! In fact I bloody love you, Pat, in fact I bloody want to marry you.'

Silence. Her mouth was hanging open, her eyes were huge. What had he said? Had he meant it? Or had he trapped himself?

Well, not for her sake. She wouldn't do that to a man, not ever. She could hope, though. She could hope.

He shrugged. He shook his shoulders. And he coughed.

'Go on, gal. Turn me down, I dare you. Go on Pat. I want to make an honest woman of you. Any chance?'

Oh yes, Pat Rose could hope.

Soon after that they'd sacked him from the Navy,

was how she understood it, although she wasn't sure, she couldn't get the exact truth out of him. He said he lived in a caravan near the diving school in Portsmouth, HMS *Vernon*, most of the time, and he fell out with them because of the officers. Pat had moved to London, and she found a little flat for him, although she'd said he could move in with her if he wanted to. And when he got sick of mooching round near *Vernon* like a tramp, he got a job not far away, with an old friend called Mr Pendock.

'He thinks that I'm some sort of unsung hero,' he told her. 'He thinks the Government've let me down. It's not a great job, he flogs tables and stuff for the coffee bars, but he says do well and I can be a partner one day. He should be so bleeding lucky!'

The timing had been good, though. His ex-diving partner Syd Knowles had also sickened of the way the Navy had treated the old gang, and had become quite bolshie. He owned his own lorry, and hauled rolls of newsprint down from the paper mills in Lancashire for 'the print.' But these days when he came to Fleet Street with a load, he didn't even bother to contact him sometimes. And that was Crabb's fault, too!

'You get yourself a phone, mate, and I'll bloody ring you up. I'm not searching Soho sleazepits for a night-out chasing crumpet with the likes of you.'

'Pat's got a phone. You could ring her, you know.'

'Aye, and you could marry her. That's what you

told the lass you'd do. And you could stop chasing ten-bob tarts an' all. You're bloody past it, mate. Wise up! That woman's worth her weight in gold.'

Looking at his snoring face beside her now, Pat Rose battled with a small despair. She was still in touch with Syd, they had become real friends. Sometimes when he was doing the London run he looked her out, and they had a drink or two in the sort of pub where Lionel wouldn't be, and they told each other things. Communed. Syd was a gentleman, and married to a woman she spoke to on the phone in Lancashire if she was feeling down. Joan. They had children, too. Syd looked out for her.

Children, for Pat Rose, was sadly not a question any more. She would admit to 'nearly forty' and Lionel was a good bit older. Then there was his drinking, and the diabetes, and the asthma. She had joked once that he needed oxygen to just get up the stairs, let alone for swimming underwater, and he had stayed sulking in his little grubby flat for days. He could be touchy sometimes, Lionel. He could get very hurt.

But the real despair was something that she feared was looming up on her. She'd heard from the neighbours that men had come to call, unknown men with classy accents who'd been sniffing round her house, men they thought might be detectives, maybe, or something to do with what was held to be his 'secret life.' However much she scoffed at such rumours, she couldn't still their wagging tongues.

Which was another reason, Lionel claimed, he had to stay away from her place – then burst into his infectious laughter.

'The idea I've got a secret life,' he hooted. 'Ridiculous.'

She did not think it was ridiculous at all. She suspected his whole life was a secret. He'd been to some very funny places. He knew some very funny men.

'I love it here with you,' he said. He held her hand. He looked into her eyes. 'But I need my freedom, Pat, you know that, love. It's more than just a place I kip, my little pad – it's there to keep me safe, it's my sort of refuge. And if you don't like it, love... well...'

This time Pat let Lionel sleep on, as so many times before. The bad dreams had faded, he was at peace again. But she was not, and it was getting harder. She thought that he was keeping something from her, that something bad was going on.

She didn't think that she could stand it too much longer. She wondered how he'd get along without her. When he woke up, maybe she'd kick him out. She meant it.

Two

Lionel Crabb could dream in cars as well as in Pat's bed, and a few days later his brain raised up the demons as he jounced drunkenly home from Soho in an early morning taxi. This time the dream involved Syd Knowles, and it was split between the warm black Mediterranean and the chilly waters round Portsmouth and the Isle of Wight.

The details, and the sense of terror, were as fluid as the running tide, and the timescale came and went in giant swoops, from wartime till the present day. Sometimes he was dressed in Navy issue overalls, baggy and waterlogged, sometimes in a skintight rubber suit like an Italian, svelte and virile. Likewise his feet: at moments in flexible long fins, at others battered plimsolls, weighted with lumps of lead.

In the Med, where he had started diving, he had sported a long, twisted, deadly knife when underwater, while Syd had favoured a shorter dagger. Neither of them had had to kill with it, although they had been trained to do so, but each could prise off or disable limpet mines. On land, in messes at Gib or Leghorn or Malta, his knife had transformed itself into a stick, hand-made by an Arab craftsman, with a highly-polished cane, and silver hilt engraved elaborately with a golden crab.

In this dream, now, as the squeaky Austin taxi bounced along the tired, rutted roads of post-war London, he relived the last dive the men had done together. It had been a year ago and Syd Knowles had only got it thanks to him. It had been a Navy Intelligence commission, and the cheapskates had figured it could be a one-man job, as befitted peacetime. Two hundred quid to Crabb, and pay his own fares down to Pompey. He had been outraged.

'Bollocks to that,' he'd said to Sydney. 'You still got your lorry, mate? Pick me up in London, take us both down to *Vernon* – they'll organise the gear for us – and afterwards we'll go out on the bash, okay? I'll buy your petrol and forty bars on top. How does that sound?'

'Diesel,' said Syd. 'It's not a bleeding Morris Minor. And how much are you getting for the job, you tight sod?'

'It's fifty five, and five more for my trouble, son. Would I do you down?'

'Aye, you would. You'd screw your dear old bloody mother. Never mind. I'll do it. What's the job?'

On paper, it had been easy. A piece of piss, a cakewalk. There was going to be a fleet review, and the Russians had been persuaded to come and fly the flag. Officially they were allies; they'd helped us win the war, ha bloody ha. The world was nuclear these days, and the Reds were faced up to the Yankees across what Churchill called the Iron Curtain. One false move and World War Three would start.

The Russkies were only sending one big ship, though, a cruiser called the *Sverdlov*. As a threat to a modern navy not a threat at all, although you wouldn't say that to an Ivan, would you? Navy Intelligence claimed she could manoeuvre a bit too smartish for an old design, and maybe had some underwater mods. Syd and Lionel Crabb were going to take a little look.

On paper it was easy, but in real life horrible. The water was full of muck and rubbish, and it was nighttime and the tide was running hard. Syd Knowles was knackered – he'd driven down from Blackburn via London – and Crabbie was half-pissed. They'd both got a bollocking off the officer from *Vernon* who thought he was in charge, and they'd both reacted badly. Divers had their own code. They didn't get pushed around by jumped-up Sawdust Samsons who knew three-fifths of bugger all.

Worst of all, in Crabbie's taxi dream, the horrors seized him by the throat underneath the bulging belly of the *Sverdlov*, and almost killed him. The South Coast tide transformed into the freezing winter waters off Gibraltar, and two Italians came from nowhere, fast and agile in their skin-tight suits and fins. And Syd was gone, Syd Knowles who had been at his side, another hapless Briton in his baggy overalls and pumps. The amateurs. The warriors dressed up as dustbin men.

It was not real, though, and as Syd swam back into his view – the real Syd Knowles, his mate, in the real frogman gear the boffins had copied off the Eyeties – Lionel twisted a valve and injected a blast of pure oxygen into this mouth and lungs. His head cleared, and they saw a cavity in the bottom of the Russian cruiser. A mystery cavity. Had Navy Intelligence been right? Had they struck gold?

Not a lot. In the increased rushing of the ebb, getting low on oxygen, expending muscle-energy hand over fist, they crawled into the cavity and discovered zilch. Maybe the outer hatchway of an airlock frogmen might use for exit and ingress, but maybe just a rusted, useless bit of hull. They were getting sick of it, and exhausted. And Lionel wanted liquor – badly.

He was no longer sure if he was still in his nightmare, but everything, in an instant, came to a juddering, swooping halt.

'Come on, mate!' the taxi driver shouted. 'Wakey-wakey, rise and shine! You're home now, Mister. Buckingham bleeding Palace! Oi!'

Crabb, in his snazzy clubbing clothes, almost

fell out of the cab into the gutter. But he wasn't that drunk, and the dream was gone. The relief was wonderful. As the fare was only eight and six he gave the man a ten-bob note, and waved away the change. He'd had a good night. It all came back to him. He'd won £12 and he'd even got a little feel off Gaynor. And he hadn't drowned...

It wasn't far to his front door, but he had a bit of trouble with the key. Inside, he breathed the smell of home without much pleasure, and grabbed the newel post before tackling the stairs. Maybe he *was* that drunk. Maybe he was getting past it, like Pat had said.

There was a new smell, though, a different one, and he knew immediately he was not alone. He heard a noise above him. A creak; the sound of breathing. Jesus! Someone had broken in.

Crabb was a short man, but he wasn't short of courage. He favoured tweed suits, a waistcoat and a monocle, and of course the smart cane with crustacean handle. And beneath the handle, his secret weapon. It was a swordstick.

No need to whip the blade out yet. He pushed himself upright, reached for the light switch in the dark, and flicked it on. At the stair-top there was a human being.

'You bastard!' bellowed Lionel Crabb. 'You've taken on more than you can chew this time! Just show your bloody self and die!'

The intruder, bathed in light, looked alone and vulnerable. No gun, no club, no knife. And he was in a suit, well-cut, dark blue.

'Eh up,' he said, mildly. 'How goes it, flower? I think they've got a little job for you. Are you up to do a lickle bit of swimming?'

'Syd, you bastard!' Crabbie said. 'You'll give me bleeding kittens. What the bloody hell?'

Pat had been right. There was something funny going on.

Three

Unlike Lionel Crabb, Knowles had kept in contact with the secret services, working on the theory they might want to use him for something, some day. Although he found the top men vile, he couldn't get enough of them – even their accents fascinated him. They laughed at his quite openly, because he came from Blackburn, while to him they were like parrots in a farting festival.

Also unlike Crabbie, Syd thought of the main chance. He'd worked his arse off to get his own lorry, and all the hours known to God to make a living in the haulage trade. Not unusual after the war, because the scrapyards were full of ex-Army wagons, and some could be picked up for a song. Some didn't last long and some were death-traps but Syd was a good mechanic. He chose a Bedford, and later upgraded to an ERF with a Gardner engine. He loved it.

So when the cloak-and-dagger boys needed him, they found him easily – they had his number. The call came from the office of Nick Elliott, the London station chief for MI6. A hard-voiced woman told Syd curtly, 'you don't need to know my name,' and demanded to be put in touch with Buster Crabb.

'Buster what?' said Syd, offended. 'Ain't never heard of him. That's a funny sort of name, chook.'

The 'chook' caused total outrage. He could almost hear her anger rising down the phone.

'Excuse me!' she said. 'Do you know to whom you're talking? Do you have any idea at all?'

'Do I buggery,' he said. 'Do you?'

'I beg your pardon! I most certainly do not!'

'So sod off then, you cheeky bitch. Buster bloody Crabb, my bloody arse.'

He put the phone down in its cradle and smiled across the living room at his wife.

She shook her head.

'You never learn do you?' she said. 'Of course she knows. She rang you up, you pillock! You'll get in trouble one day, you will.' She laughed.

'You're funny though, I will say that. Who were it?'

'Some stuck-up tart sniffing round for Crabbie. If it's urgent they can try again, so sod 'em. I think I'd better warn Pat though, don't you?'

He thought he wouldn't mention it to Crabb, though. Crabb was bored to death of civvy life, and if the call could get him out of flogging furniture, he'd jump at it.

Which might well be the bloody death of him.

Four

The search for Crabb had been set on when Sir Anthony Eden, the Prime Minister, learned that his long effort at a diplomatic coup was paying out in spades. After months of delicate negotiations, a naval visit had been agreed – three Russian warships into Portsmouth, with the highest of top brass.

'Nikita Khrushchev and Nikolai Bulganin,' Sir Norman Brook had told him. 'Good heavens, it's the prize to end all prizes! Party Secretary and Prime Minister, in their most prestigious cruiser, with an escort of destroyers. The Americans will be green with envy!'

Sir Norman, although Secretary to the Cabinet, was still a cautious man, who was looked upon with deep suspicion at the very top, having actually gone only to a grammar school. Ninety per cent of men in highest Government had come from public schools, and almost all of them from Eton. Brook was an oik, a rank outsider.

'You understand, sir, that this visit will need the utmost delicacy?' he said. 'The Russian bear is, shall we say, a prey to paranoia. They will see themselves as vulnerable, and assume that we'll be spying on them from the outset. I trust you do agree, Prime Minister, that the secret services be reined in?'

Sir Anthony (although an Eton man himself) was also cautious, and not half the fool his coevals chose to think he was. When British warships had visited Vladivostok not so long ago, divers had churned up the waters all around them like a school of porpoises, and the Russians had denied that they were spying until they were blue in the face. Eden had chosen to think that that was funny, but knew damn well the Russians, if they saw activity in Portsmouth, would not agree.

'An incident,' he murmured. 'Norman, you are right.' He gave the dour man a dour smile. 'Ivan can be a rumbustious opponent, even on the friendliest occasions. For the foreseeable future, this must be our secret, and ours alone. Do we agree?'

Brook's smile grew thinner yet.

'Indeed we do. Except that I believe some elements in MI6 have sniffed the breeze already. Fleming might only put his wilder ideas into unpleasant books now, but some of his remaining friends still seem to think such fantasies are real.'

'Fleming? Should I know the name?'

You should, thought Norman Brook, you're meant to have your finger on the pulse, you are Prime Minister. He let it go, however.

'Ian Fleming, sir. Naval Intelligence Division in the war, now peddling half-truths on the Sunday Times. Writes pulp novels, sees everything in terms of blood and sex.'

'Ah,' said Eden. He did know Fleming, he remembered – and would rather he did not. He liked drinking too much whisky, seducing secretaries, and all the vices common to Durnford, a prep school that seemed dedicated to wrecking little boys. Kicked out of Eton, ditto Sandhurst with galloping VD, and the destroyer of Lord

Rothermere's marriage by rampant cuckoldry. A most unsavoury man.

'Indeed,' he said. 'But offices, as we know, are notorious rumour mills. Our job, Brook – or your job may I say – is to bear down on this like a ton of bricks. No more rumours, no more plots, and absolutely no more silly talk about spying on the ships. Find out for me immediately who's been spreading this, deny it to the hilt, and point out to the highest echelons that there will be no funny business, none at all.'

'I will, sir. Right to the top. Sir John, Nick Elliott—'

'Whoever. The Russians will come here unmolested, and remain here in the same condition. No bedrooms will be wired up for sound, no clandestine searches of the ships by surface boats or underwater. Nikita Khrushchev looks something like an ugly new-born baby in a certain light, and this time he will be treated like one. I want nothing – *nothing* – that could provoke an incident. To all intents and purposes, Brook, the Russians are our allies. And will be regarded so.'

'Thugs and murderers to a man, but our best of friends,' the Cabinet Secretary responded drily. 'One wonders, sometimes, if this is what we won the war for.'

'And paid so much in blood and treasure. Yes.'

When Eden's edict came to MI6 it caused consternation – and the makings of open-faced revolt. The fact that Brook delivered it drove such reactions underground, however, and double-quick. Sir Norman was despised and hated by the men who ran the nation's foreign secret service – the men who called themselves the Robber Barons – and like any mafia they had a rule of silence. Not only Sicilians lived by *omerta*.

Nicholas Elliott, supremo in the London station, had already heard about the Russian visit through Fleming, and asked to talk about it face-to-face with him. It was long before midday when they met up, but Fleming called for whisky. Nick did not demur.

'Brook's an utter pill,' he said. 'Do you know, Fleming, he says nothing must be done by any of us. It's the good old English way, the land of wasted opportunities. Three Russians tied up in Portsmouth Harbour like sitting ducks and they're out of bounds? Who was it said God's dead? The man was bloody right.'

'It was Friedrich Nietzsche,' said Ian Fleming, deadpan. 'A German intellectual. You wouldn't have heard of him.'

'Ha bloody ha,' replied Nick Elliott. 'You were my fag I might remind you, Fleming; I taught you everything you know. Except your liking for Hunnish practices, if what I hear's correct. Too many beatings in the master's room, was it?'

They were smiling easily, warmed by whisky and their shared experience. Both men had suffered from a violent education. Neither of them thought of it as suffering.

'Oh come off it, Nicholas. Durnford was your prep school, wasn't it? No doors on the shitters by headmaster's order, and your bollocks used for bonbons by the under-gardeners. What precisely do you mean by "nothing must be done?" What sort of nothing?'

'I mean the edict comes straight from bloody Anthony, our dear Prime Minister. The only thing he did at Eton, as I recall it, was win prizes for Divinity, and if he's not a queer I'm Mussolini. Rab Butler once called him something on those lines, certainly. Can't recall precisely what.'

Fleming smiled round his whisky glass.

'It was "half a mad baronet, half a beautiful woman." It's in my notebook for future use. Maybe Eden went a bit too far with bum-onomics after lights out.'

Elliott tutted.

'Don't be crude, old man. There isn't any evidence on that score, I do assure you. And I can smell a poof at three hundred yards, like any other sort of deviant. That's how I know about your yearning for the whip!'

Fleming was relaxed. He did not believe his friend necessarily knew his private pleasures, and in any case he did not care. Elliott had his secrets too. His dependency on drink was legendary, and some of his trusted friends were trusted by no other thinking person. He'd make a splendid villain one day, in a spy book. Plausible, charming and rather dim.

'But precisely, if I may continue,' said Elliott, 'the order came from Eden, and he said specifically we weren't to even think about spying on the ships. To get Khrushchev and Bulganin to come to England in the first place he sees as some sort of major triumph, and his advisors have told him any mess-up could blow up in our faces. Upset the Yankees for a start. And make the Cold War hot again, in one fell swoop.'

'That sounds like Norman,' Fleming laughed. 'Born mealy-mouthed, brought up mealy-mouthed, and now he's secretary to a Cabinet of cowards.

Sometimes one wishes we had men like Khrushchev in command. Might not look a charmer, but he personally murdered dozens of his closest comrades getting to the top. Firm but fair!'

'No need to over-egg, old man. Kim Philby says the actual count of brains blown out was just eleven, and Kim never makes mistakes about the Russians. You'd do well to let him help you with your penny dreadfuls. Give them a bit of class!'

Fleming was unfazed.

'Khrushchev can have killed as many as he damn well pleases for my money, but for once Eden might be right. That Soviet abortion's head is stuffed with evil genius, my friend – and if you kick a hornet's nest you can get stung.'

'Now who's mealy-mouthed?' said Elliott. 'I think your first assessment's right – Eden's a coward and a queer. And I'll tell you this much – I'm not going to let the opportunity pass us by. Khrushchev's a peasant from the sticks, and I'm going to spy on him. No argument.'

'Well, you won't hear one from me,' said Ian Fleming, emptying his glass. 'Will you use frogmen? They're good at cutting throats. Such a very, very sexy trade.'

Elliott laughed.

'I've already tried, but the woman I chose to do the first approach made a total balls-up. I take it you remember Crabb?'

'Ah, Buster. Bit of a lush, bit of a buffoon, and an aficionado of the grubby in a woman, if I recall. But you don't get the George Medal by playing by the rules, do you? What did he say?'

'You're not listening, Fleming. We haven't found him yet. Got another man trying, though, when I finally get to speak to him. What they call in the trade Buster's "oppo" apparently. Queer folk, the lower orders, what? Man called Knowles.'

'I know Syd Knowles. Another damn good diver. And "oppo" means his opposite number, you ignoramus. If Buster's gone to ground, he'll flush him out – just tell him that there's cash in it for him. He's from Lancashire is Sydney, but he's as tight as any Yorkshire Tyke. He'll do "owt fer brass!"'

'You're rather low yourself, Fleming. I'm surprised my pater let you in his school. And I've got a smarter lady on the job of hooking Knowles this time, not some dried up old civil service stick. She's a sweetie, actually. I'll make damn sure you never get to meet her.'

Fleming laughed.

'Don't mind me, old man, I don't go short. I'll sniff her out in any case, you mark my words. But come on though, enough dancing round the unimportant things – how about another little drink?'

Five

The 'smart young lady' Elliott had in mind for 'hooking' Knowles was a new girl in the office, whose form he'd been assessing for some time. He referred to her, without a hint of irony, as 'my beautiful assistant.' Her actual name was neither that nor 'little sweetie,' but Marion Wilson, recently promoted from the typing pool.

Aware that bypassing the Prime Minister was not without its dangers, Elliott moved with unusual caution to assess and brief her for the task. She needed, above all, to be quick on the uptake. And discreet.

'First off,' he told her, 'I need to know what the PM has in mind, and who's doing the liaising. Between him and Norman Brook there's layers of bureaucracy the Soviets themselves would appreciate, and it will foul everything if the fact we're interested leaks out. Do you understand me?'

She flashed a smile. She was a small, neat girl, classed in the department as a 'poppet'. Nick liked his helpers nubile. They had potential in so many ways.

'I think I do, sir. And isn't Sir Norman putting in a snooper?'

Elliott laughed.

'Indeed he is,' he said. 'But officially, he will be called a Foreign Office Advisor.

Mr Eden, it appears, doesn't trust us to do right by these Russians, and this is Brook's ruse to keep us under supervision. So if I ask you to contact a frogman for me, it is completely innocent, of course. And absolutely between the two of us.'

'Oh absolutely, sir.' Her smile grew very impish. 'Would it be the man who did the *Sverdlov* job last year, by any chance? Commander Crabb?'

'Good heavens, what a memory. But there is another man as well.'

'Ah.' Marion was disappointed. 'And he'll be the one you want, I suppose? Bother!' He patted her on the shoulder.

'He's not half so memorable, Miss Wilson, I promise you. Name of Knowles, and in comparison to Crabb completely normal. Buster dresses like a fighting cock, drinks like a fish, and gambles like a bookie's dream. Got kicked out of the service a year or two ago, and fought it like a madman despite it was done to save his life on grounds of age and health. Strange little fellow.'

'Ah,' said Marion. 'I know about the drink. He's disgraced himself a time or two in the grandees' bar is what I heard. Something to do with spats and a swordstick, one of the girls said. And check suits and big plus fours, maybe a pork-pie hat? Definitely bizarre.'

Elliott stifled laughter.

'The story is – and I hope to God it isn't true – that little Buster sometimes turns up on assignations dressed as a frogman. No, honestly – complete with flippers.'

'Assignations? What, you don't mean—'

'Indeed I do! On dates! To impress the ladies! Quite shocking, really.'

If the poppet was shocked, she hid it very well. She smiled her neatest smile.

'He sounds a fright, sir. And is the swordstick true, as well? All I can say is, he must be a jolly good frogman *indeed* to make up for all that!'

She brought them coffee, and they got down to cases. The files confirmed that Syd

Knowles was also retired, though many years younger than Buster Crabb, who was forty seven. Crabb had been the instigator on the *Sverdlov* job, and had shelled out cash to Sydney from his own fee.

'Any addresses? Contact details?'

She leafed through papers.

'Still nothing for Crabb. Reading between the lines he was in a mighty huff with us, and seems to have gone to ground. He was paid off quite suddenly, only two years after he'd been made up to commander.'

Elliott remembered. Crabb's flamboyance had got too much for some of his superiors, as had his drinking. He'd been described as a strutting gamecock with ideas above his station, in one memo. And had sometimes claimed he'd gone to public school. Embarrassing.

'Our people have snooped around an old address, apparently,' continued Marion. 'It was his lady friend's, maybe, but they seem to have got nowhere anyway. Knowles is still in Blackburn, though, with the same phone number.'

'I know. I put Maude Simpkins onto it, before I came to you. She merely managed to…well, let's just say another good contact ruined. Women.'

She did not even raise an eyebrow.

'I'll have a go myself, sir. See if I can work my female charms. Maude is—' She stopped. She felt disloyal.

'Rather short in that department,' finished Elliott. 'I'm expecting far greater things from my Maid Marion.' He smiled. 'Knowles delivers newsprint to London from the north, they tell me. If he's due down in a day or so set up a meeting, and if he's not, we'll bring him by train, expenses paid. Plus a fee. I want him, poppet. Extremely badly.'

'But you still want Crabb, sir? Or—'

'Of course I still want Crabb. I want the pair of them, they're a great team. They worked together in the war – Gibraltar, Malta, Livorno, everywhere. If a Russian lady's bottom needs feeling, we couldn't find a better pair of hands. Oh dammit, Marion. That was crass.'

'Wash your mouth out, sir,' she laughed. 'Would you like another cup of coffee?'

'Sweet,' Nick Elliott replied.

Six

In two more days Miss Wilson had found Sydney, and he agreed to track down Crabb. But before he would divulge any information, he said, he must meet Elliott at a venue of his own choosing, which Marion thought impertinent. He offered her no choice, however, and she was forced to accept a pub in Fleet Street.

To her surprise, Nick Elliott was not put out. Like many of the very rich, he liked to think he had 'the common touch'. It struck him as quaint that Knowles turned up in overalls, and genuinely disturbing that this working man was neither overtly patriotic nor keen to 'earn an honest bob'. He seemed strangely concerned, indeed, for the older diver's health.

'Now look, sir,' he said at one point – he would not call him Nick at any price – 'I think you're off the beam on this one, if you don't mind me saying so. You're talking early April, you're talking bloody freezing in that harbour, you're talking a man who's been around a bit.'

'Of course he has,' Nick blustered. 'He's the best, the *crème de* ... he's the best. Of course he's been around, that's why we want him for this job. This job's important, man. It is vital. It is—'

He stopped himself. The pub was called the Tipperary and it was full of roughneck printers. Rising off them, he could feel something like embarrassment at his presence. And dislike.

'Do you know how old he is, sir? Lionel? He's bloody nearly fifty. I'm too old for diving and I'm only thirty four. And he smokes Player's, too – we call 'em coffin nails. He smokes a hundred of the bastard things a day.'

'I've seen his medicals.'

Elliott stopped. He'd wrong-footed himself once more. Too much knowledge.

'Yes, you're right,' he said. 'He does smoke a bit too much, but that's his choice, surely? We're fighting men, we're not his nanny for God's sake. There's a bloody war on.'

Knowles did not laugh, he didn't have to. He sensed Elliott blushing in the gloom.

'A war by any other name?' he said. 'But round here, though, there's some who reckon Russia's not the enemy. Some of the newsprint that I haul gets the Daily Herald printed on it. Aye, it's true that, think on.'

Elliott felt class tension rising in his breast. He'd gone to Eton, for God's sake; his father was headmaster! Their ethos was to make the world a better place for everybody, class and wealth notwithstanding. These people, these people… He crushed the thought.

'Look,' he said, 'I know it's not ideal, Syd. He is an older man. He retired some time ago, but—'

'He *was* retired. On grounds of age!'

'Okay. On grounds of age. But he fought it like a tiger! He said that he was going to try and sue us! God's sake, Sydney, give the man a fu— Give the man a flipping chance, can't you?'

'He's a lush. An alcoholic. He drinks whisky like there's no tomorrow. He took me to a top-notch club once, to introduce me to "new friends". Friends! God spare the bleeding mark! Poofters! Ponces! Fellow bleeding travellers! He told me he was going to de…'

Knowles stopped himself. He had been going to say defect, which on one drunken evening he had begun to half believe. But Crabbie was a mate, who had risked his life a thousand times to fight for England. He was not a traitor. He would never be.

'Going to what?' said Nick Elliott. 'Good heavens, man, were you going to say defect? But—'

'Depressed!' snapped Knowles. 'He was going to get depressed! He thought that he'd got shit on. Then he met these fairies and they took him to posh parties, and they filled him full of booze and talked about the Russkies like they was Jesus Christ incarnate. Turncoats, all of them, and the worst one was the poshest of the lot. Blunt, they called him, Anthony Blunt. No they didn't – they called him the fucking Queen Mother! Treachery or what?'

He'd raised his voice, but luckily the Tipperary was filling up and the noise was at its height. Elliott knew much about the homosexuals who thronged the secret services, and it worried him a little; but he also knew that Blunt was a sound man, not an ounce of communism in him, or of treachery. It worried him more, actually, that an oaf like Knowles had got to hear such things. And might spread them round in the wrong circles.

He took a draught of Trumans' bitter and longed for the taste of claret. *The things I do for England...*

'Buster, as you say, could be a thought depressive,' he said, carefully. 'In fact – and this is strictly confidential, Sydney – he was prone to hallucinations, in a minor way. On top of all that booze, perhaps—'

'He couldn't get a fucking job!' Syd snapped. 'That's the long and short of it, cocker! He couldn't get a job and they chucked him on the scrapheap after promoting him. And now you need the bastard back, you'll throw him to the dogs. You'll murder him!'

Even Nicholas Elliott's legendary urbanity was being tested, but he worked at it for another half an hour or more. He denigrated all his equals – and superiors – and agreed with every wild and ill-considered slander Knowles could sling at him and them. It was men like Crabb who were the most important ones, he insisted with vehemence, men like Crabb who were the salt of the earth, men like Crabb who carried the true banner.

The upshot was – he concluded in true Eton debating style – that Crabb would want to help his country, would understand the risk to all that he held dearest in the world. But only if a friend like Knowles would act as honest go-between. Elliott worked very, very hard.

And finally, they shook on it.

Thus it came about that Syd agreed to tell MI6 where Crabb lived and help persuade him that his country needed him again. Neither as stupid nor as honest as Elliott confidently assumed, he negotiated a large financial settlement, and another one for Crabb.

He further said that he would make the first approach – the 'old mates' gambit – and persuade him to do the job, however long it took. Then he lied that he had urgent work to do, more or less pushed Elliott out into the street, and took another pint of Trumans, with a whisky chaser. He sat down at a corner table to have a think.

Crabb *had* talked of defecting, but it had never been more than fury at the way the wankers treated him. In his years as kingpin of the world of secret frogmen he'd got close to some pretty unlikely people, up to and including Mountbatten, the First

Sea Lord, who was plain 'Dickie' to him, or so he claimed. He'd let himself be sucked into the highest echelons most eagerly, then let it turn his head.

They were all so fucking posh, so far out of his class. Plums in their mouths the size of donkeys' knackers, and Crabbie didn't seem to know that they were mocking him. They took him to restaurants where the food would make your eyes pop out, then on to clubs stuffed full of shirt-lifters. He'd dragged Syd along once, and they'd fallen out about it. It wasn't hard to fall out with Crabb when the drink was on him. Pat Rose said that he was often suicidal.

The top gun of the poofter gang had been the one they called Queen Mum. Lanky as a streak of piss, face like a broken violin. He knew Picasso, he'd told Syd, and his face when Syd had asked him who the fuck Picasso was had been a picture. He was a berk from way back; a gold-plated Berkeley Hunt, and maybe even seemed to fancy Crabbie for himself. Good luck there, mate, thought Sydney: his piles are like a bunch of fucking blackberries!

Reds the lot of them: Commies, MPs, one guy apparently the boss of MI5. Knowles took another swig. Crabb had been so bitter about the way the service treated him.

'Best fucking diver in the world I am,' he'd said one night, when he'd had his usual skinful and a half. 'You know that, don't you, Syd? And those bastards think I'm past it. I tell you what, if they don't give me something soon, I'm off to fucking Moscow. They need frogmen over there – theirs are total crap. If something don't come up soon, it's the Soviets or suicide. Straight!'

Yeah, bollocks, Sydney thought. You ought to watch yourself, old son. If you really did try to defect, they'd kill you. All your top-drawer chums would slit your fucking throat. English heroes are for England; they don't export. Just watch your fucking mouth.

He didn't really believe it, though. Crabb was just pissed off. Crabb was a patriot, and he always would be. And now Elliott was offering big money, so Syd would talk his old chum into just one last mad job for them. He'd told the snobby Secret Service twat he would. He'd promised him. Although he knew that it was tantamount to murder.

Syd Knowles left the Tipperary as happy as a little lark. He had been lying.

Seven

Kim Philby was no longer one of the Robber Barons, but he got to hear of the secret operation just as he got to hear of everything. Although no less a personage than the Foreign Secretary, Harold Macmillan, had told the House of Commons Philby was not the 'so-called Third Man of British traitors', there were elements in MI6 who still distrusted him. The head of London, however, was not one of them. Nick Elliott had been his closest friend for years.

'Good God, old man,' he'd said when the storm first broke, 'all they've got against you is that you drank with Burgess and Maclean before they joined the Reds. Which is true for all of us! Hang on in there, chum. I'll back you all the way.'

Philby, though, had chosen to resign – 'for my honour as a gentleman' – which had only made Elliott trust and revere him more. After that, any suspicion of his best chum was outrageous.

'Third man, fourth man, fifth – well, what a load of tosh,' he told people. 'Burgess went to probe some hairy Russian arseholes, and Maclean's just a drip. Philby's been my friend since we were almost in short

45

trousers; I'd trust my life with him. Good God alive – I'd even trust my wife!'

That, some men considered, would have been a great mistake. Others, mainly of MI5, thought that their *sons* would be at greater risk; but MI5 were never gentlemen, and none of them had even been to Eton. Nick Elliott's father did not let just any riffraff in!

Crabb's name came up between the two men over drinks one night, on the understanding the operation was so sensitive that he should not even hint of it to anyone. Kim smiled acknowledgement of the compliment. And revealed the man was not unknown to him.

'What, old Buster? Christ, is he still with us? I thought he'd drunk himself to death aeons ago. I could never decide if he was absurdly brave or merely thick. Swordstick. That fucking swordstick! A talented buffoon in spats and monocle.'

It was early in the evening, so they were still at the cocktail stage, their food already ordered. Then it would be wine, then port. Then they would repair to the grandees' bar, replete and happy, and try some brandy, or a malt or three. Two friends catching up; they were not drinking seriously.

'Oh, don't do him down, don't do him down,' said Elliott. 'I revere men like him, in some ways. Rough edges, maybe, but salt of the earth, absolutely. I mean the clothes, yes. You've heard about the frogman's suit as evening wear, of course? But apart from little things like that, Kim—'

'Little things!' Kim Philby howled. 'Good God, Nick, I'd like to hear a female opinion on that sort of "little thing!" Next you'll tell me rubber sheets!'

Nick was uncomfortable.

'He's a hero, Kim.' he said. 'He really is a hero, his bravery is quite extraordinary. But he wishes that he—'

'Was one of us. Exactly. He needs to think that we all like him, that we actually admire the buffoon. He couldn't even make it in the Merchant Navy. And that accent he puts on, for God's sake!'

'The point is,' said Elliott stiffly, 'that he is not only still with us, but potentially he can even save the nation, if Ivan should ever want to go to war with us again. He is phenomenal.'

'Deniable, as well,' smirked Philby. 'And entirely dispensable. If everything goes right he can be a hero, and if he drops dead of old age and too much smoking, no one will give a flying fuck. He is, my friend, perfection! Congratulations.'

'Your cynicism surprises me,' said Elliott. 'But joking to one side, he won't drop dead, what do you take me for? They—'

'Breed 'em tough down in the gutter!' Kim interrupted. 'So what exactly is this job? What do you want him for?'

One never talked of work outside the office, but Nick knew Kim Philby to the bottom of his soul. He could tell him anything.

'Tight one,' he said. 'And we're defying orders from the top no less, the damned PM. He's put a blanket ban on it, so if we cock up there'll be hell to pay – I'll be bumped down to the third eleven, even.'

The food needed attention and for a few minutes they sipped and chewed.

'You see,' continued Elliott at last, 'Eden sees it as a coup. He's persuaded the Reds to bring their navy on a visit, a gesture to defuse the Cold War tensions. Our Naval Int boys are certain some of their ships have had mods done to their hulls, but last time one came by we didn't get a proper look. This time the ships are mooring up against the harbour wall in Pompey. Lambs to the slaughter.'

Philby drank carefully.

'Top work, old boy,' he said, admiringly. 'I take it you're too modest to tell the whole truth, though, aren't you? Who's idea was it?'

A self-deprecating chuckle.

'Not mine, I promise you. Eden did it off his own bat, apparently. What's more he's got the top brass coming, too. Khrushchev and Bulganin, the icing on the cake of State! Their rooms at Claridge's will have more bugs in than a dhobi-wallah's doodahs. It's the one thing that the duffers in MI5 do rather well.'

'It couldn't have been our Anthony's idea, though, the man's an utter pill. It smells like Macmillan's hand to me. Or brain, at least.'

'No, I swear it's Anthony's. Because listen to this: when I said I'd put our best men on it, I got a massive wigging straight back from Norman Brook. "No monitoring. No tapped telephones. No ladies of the night with microphones tucked up their frilly bits". Then Sinclair called me in himself to rub it in.'

'Oh, Sir John,' Philby said dismissively. 'Man's a disgrace, the worst "C" ever. And what did he say? Nothing interesting, I suppose?'

Before the night was out, then, Philby had every detail of the operation known so far. And when Knowles had brought Buster Crabb on side, Elliott promised him, he'd be told that, too.

'And what if wee Anthony gets wind?' asked Kim. 'Even he might have a pair of balls inside those fancy trews, you know. He could throw his handbag at you, Nick! Right royal tantrum! Like a proper queen.'

Elliott drained his last balloon of brandy. They'd had enough to kill a horse, but neither of them was even slurring.

'He'll never know,' he said. 'Pa may have let him have a place at Eton, but the only one he ever bothered there was God. All that tosh he's always spouting about peace, as well. Disgraceful.

The trouble is with men like him, they just don't understand. They think that Russians are like normal human beings, not savages. But you know what we're dealing with, don't you? You know what swine they really are.'

Philby rolled his eyes expressively.

'Oh don't I just! Neanderthals from a bygone age! You're right, old friend, this is what we've got to do to save old England. Find out all ghastly Ivan's ghastly secrets! For once, dear Anthony has hit the bullseye.'

'They say he's got some sort of drug addiction,' Elliott put in. 'Not ghastly Ivan, our dear leader Eden. Mistress Prim's on so much medication, apparently, that he never sleeps. He's as nervous as a kitten. Paranoid. He hardly even drinks.'

He laughed aloud.

'I don't know what he's taking,' he added, 'but I hope to God they never force some down my throat! Which reminds me – would you like another one? Just for the road.'

'Well,' said Philby. 'I was beginning to think you were never going to ask.'

Eight

The night that Sydney tracked him down and proved the Yale lock useless in the good old-fashioned way, Crabbie had gone from drunk to sober by halfway up the stairs. He held his blade in front of him, still sheathed, and licked his lips. Here was Syd, out of the blue. And Crabb needed another whisky.

His voice was not a deep one, but he cleared his throat, and pitched it low and scratchy. Quite easy on a hundred snout a day.

'Sydney,' he said. 'You bastard. What brings you here? I've just had a bloody dream about you!'

The suit, when he saw it closer, was not so well cut after all. Not exactly demob, but not one of Burton's finest either; the tailor of taste didn't go in for faded blue with bald spots. In his spats and natty beige, Lionel Crabb felt superior. Suddenly, it pleased him.

'Bloody hell,' he said. 'You never were a snappy dresser, were you? You look a proper sight.'

Knowles let out a bark of laughter.

'Teks one to know one, lad,' he said. 'You still doin' fancy dress? Were that in your dream an'all?'

From anyone else, this might have caused a

ruction, but they went back a long, long way. Crabb grinned and clung on to the banister for a moment. The smell of booze rose past him up the stair.

'You got a fag, have you? I must've dropped mine in the cab. Bloody drivers nowadays. They don't know how to treat a lady.'

Knowles was taller than Crabb, but he bent down to hand him to the top. It was acceptable help, apparently, and the cigarette packet made it more so. Crabb got one in his mouth as to the manner born, flaming up his Yankee Zippo in a movement.

'Only Turf, mate, sorry,' Knowles said. 'You still on Players, are you? The tobacco that counts!'

'Turf never had a slogan, did they, Sydney? And anyone who sunk that low couldn't read in any case, present company and all that. So go on then – you think you've got a job for me? What's that all about? Don't mind me if I laugh, but you look destitute.'

They'd arrived in the living room, and Buster threw himself full-length onto the sofa. He let out a sudden alcoholic groan, then coughed. The cough went on and on. Syd Knowles sat silently.

'What it is,' he said, at last, 'well, what it is, is top brass at the SIS. You remember Elliott? Smarmy bastard that reckons he's God's gift? Says he's got a job for us, and they didn't know where to find you. Asked me to sound you out. They told me you'd retired.'

Crabb was still coughing. It took some time to stop.

'The cheeky bastards – *they* retired *me*, last year, dropped me right in it. I had to get a proper job! I'm not old!'

He coughed a little more, sucked deeply on the Turf.

'I run a furniture emporium,' he said. 'It's high class and I nearly own it. Cheeky bastards, thinking that I'm old.'

Knowles knew much more of the story than he was letting on, because of Pat Rose. Truth was, Crabb flogged tables to the café trade, from a showroom down the road. He didn't even own the tables. That was a man called Pendock, who Pat said had always had a soft spot for him.

'So making lots of lolly, I suppose? Nice.'

Things could get edgy, talking about cash, and they both rowed back. Syd slipped a quarter bottle of Scotch from his inner pocket and flashed it. Grant's. Five minutes later they were friends again. They were talking seriously.

The job they'd done in fifty-five had involved the *Sverdlov*, which was suspected by the Yanks of having had something fishy done to her. They had in fact spotted what looked like a propeller tucked up a tunnel in the hull, but the tide was running fast and murky and they'd had too little time for definites.

Both men had gone ashore exhausted, but Crabb proposed an all-night drinking session. Knowles was driving back to Lancashire and they'd fallen out.

Tonight it was Syd who had the cash, to persuade Crabb that they should do the job again. Not the same job though, a more important one, with MI6 dosh for both of them – tons of it. According to Nick Elliott it was a walkover, and vital for the country's good. They were patriots. They should jump at it. And Crabb, Syd thought, would do just that.

But Syd had made his own mind up. He looked at his oppo – coughing, smoking, sick with alcohol – and the evidence stared back at him. Cash or no cash, Lionel Crabb must never do this dive. Last time he'd swum beneath a Russian hull he'd had a death wish, and had survived. Today he was knocking at death's door. Next knock might be the Reaper. Grim.

'Thing is,' he said, 'they've got some more ships coming. One cruiser, two destroyers and they want their bottoms looking at. Far as I can see' – he improvised – 'they think we'll get the chance to stick a limpet mine or two on one of 'em. No, mate, I'm serious! Sounds daft to me, but who am I to judge? We're only infantry. We stick the mines, we cut and run – we bloody die!'

They were drinking neat scotch from china cups, and Knowles was going to finish the bottle before he broke the news. Lionel, he'd decided, Commander

Lionel Buster Crabb, GM, OBE, the drunken dwarf of Streatham, could no more dive beneath a ship in Portsmouth than he could fly.

He drained his cup and lumbered to his feet.

'Suicide,' he said. 'They must be fucking mad. They must think we've just got off the boat. Sorry, Crabbie, you're right, no danger. This one's not like that last do I got you on – it's plain impossible.'

Crabb's head was muzzy, but he was not confused.

'What d'you mean – *I'm* right?' he said, sharply. 'I never said a bleeding word. And I got *you* on the last one, if you don't mind! And watched your back every inch, you toe-rag! Limpet mines my bloody arse! You're raving! We're doing it.'

Syd Knowles was heading for the door.

'We're not, because I've nixed it, mate,' he said. 'They want to kill us and they can go and whistle up their arses. Trouble is, they'll find out where you live now, you'll have to piss them off yourself when they come knocking. I'm sorry, but I've give you warning, haven't I? Just say no, mate. Just refuse. They don't care if they fucking kill you.'

He flung the Turf packet onto the sofa.

'Just in case you're short,' he said. 'I'd smoke myself to death if I was you. Be a lot less painful, one way and the other. Honest, Crabbie. Think.'

'Oh, piss off, you yellow bastard,' Crabb muttered. 'And by the way, how did you get in here? You scum.'

'How d'you think, you drunken prat? You didn't even lock the bloody door when you went on the piss.'

'It was locked when I came back! You're a bloody liar, Knowlesy! You're a bloody lying twat!'

But he was talking to an empty room.

Nine

Like any good spymaster, Nick Elliott had staff to do the legwork, so Marion Wilson carried on with Crabb, and now and then he picked her brains. She might be middle-class but she was easy on the eye, which was what really mattered. And she was quick, and very bright.

'Crabb's had a funny life, sir, since the war,' she said one afternoon. 'I mean, he's worked for us a bit, but he's also done a lot of other things which are quite peculiar.'

'Define peculiar,' said Elliott.

She pointed at a photo on the desk between them.

'Well he looks peculiar, in any case. That cigarette, for instance. I mean, it's like the ones my Uncle Ronnie smokes. He was in the Navy. He used to roll them up himself. With sticky papers.'

'What rank was he?'

'Something in the engine room, I think. But perhaps Mr Crabb had been given it. In the files it says he smokes Player's Navy Cut.'

'Ah.' Nick smiled. 'Not just a stoker, then. Not a Woodbines man. But you were going to define peculiar, I believe?'

She coloured.

'It says here he worked as a model, which I also don't understand. I mean, my cousin wanted to be a model. But she's a ... well, she's a girl.'

'Most appropriate,' said Elliott. 'But we're modern now, it's 1956. Anything else?'

'Well, he's been an undertaker. And it says art salesmen here as well, although I guess that just means selling pictures door-to-door. My uncle—'

She saw his face. Enough of uncles.

'Now he sells furniture. Not high-class stuff. Tables and chairs to go in cafes, sort of thing, for a Mr Pendock. And what he earns I think he gets rid of a bit too quickly for his own good. Or his wife's. Well, fiancée, actually.'

'Meaning?'

What she meant was that Crabb led a life of minor chaos. He drank like a fish, gambled like a fool, and was notorious for dating tarty barmaids. He'd been married to a woman called Margaret in 1952 but it had lasted less than a year, and his current girlfriend, Pat Rose, had been engaged to him before and after that event..

'He sounds despicable. I wouldn't touch him with a barge-pole, sir. Just because he's got a swagger stick!'

'Ah yes,' said Elliott. 'The famous swordstick with the silver knob. It's tragic really, isn't it?'

She pursed her lips. He was mocking her. But then he sighed.

'He had a long war, Maid Marion, you might be too young to really understand. Commander Crabb, whatever he may look like, did things that few other men have ever done. He became a frogman before the term had even been invented.'

'I don't understand that, sir,' she said stiffly. 'The logic is beyond me, I'm afraid.'

'The Italians invented it, strange though that might seem. By the time the war started in the Mediterranean, they had miniature submarines and limpet mines and all sorts. They caused untold destruction. Men like Crabb – only the merest handful of them, with no proper equipment – were sent out there in boiler suits and plimsolls to prise off explosives they'd planted on the bottoms of our ships. They had a thoroughly unpleasant time.'

He laughed.

'It's funny, isn't it? We English think the Italians can only run away. Cowards, all of them. It's balderdash. They attacked ships in the Med seated astride torpedoes full of high explosive, breathing pure oxygen that they knew would kill them given half a chance. If Mr Crabb and Co had not caught up with them we could have lost the war.'

Marion was not capitulating.

'But oxygen *is* pure. How could it kill them?

There's nothing purer in the world is there?'

'Below thirty feet or so the pressure turns it deadly, sadly. Frogmen call it Oxygen Pete - the P for Poisoning. If they survive that, they might get the Bends by coming up too fast. Bubbles of nitrogen form in the blood, collecting at the joints. And they fill their lungs in agony before they can reach the surface. Drown. Chaps like your friend Lionel - good, low chaps who don't know how to treat a lady – had a long war and a deadly one. You may not see it, but he has a saving grace or two.'

Elliott sat back in his chair, and shook his head as if to clear it.

'I'm glad we've had this conversation, in a way – it's done me a very useful service. I'd half decided, because of bureaucratic whines about Crabb's age and health and so on, that I might try and find another man to do the job, but I've changed my mind. It's Buster, Buster all the way. And I'm sure he'll be entirely gung-ho.'

Miss Wilson blinked.

'Two years ago he was too old,' she said, carefully. 'He was forcibly retired, wasn't he?'

'So you think I'm doing wrong, do you?'

'Of course not, sir, of course not.' She paused. 'Of course I'm sure you wouldn't risk... I mean... It's just he looks so *little*, sir. So much like a...garden gnome.'

'That's sentimental twaddle, I'm afraid. Crabb

is the greatest frogman, possibly, the world has ever known. Size isn't everything, my poppet. Isn't that what they always tell you ladies?'

She began to shuffle files. She was embarrassed, but she stole a side glance at his face. He was a kindly soul, impossible to doubt it. Would he really risk this poor man's life?

'He still looks like a gnome though, sir,' she said, uncomfortably.

She tried to make a joke of it.

'Couldn't we get a little fishing rod for him out of the stores? Maybe a little pointy hat?'

He hooted. What a good idea!

Ten

Syd Knowles, two mornings later, had a much grittier meeting with Nick Elliott. He said point blank he would not do the job, and neither would 'Commander Crabb – *retired.*' He had persuaded him to turn it down himself.

'What?' said Elliott. His voice was like a stream of ice. 'You persuaded him to defy a direct order? From the Prime Minister?'

Knowles did not blink.

'It's not an order though, is it? It's a try-on and you know it. Crabb retired because they made him, and they were bloody right. He's a diabetic. He's an alcoholic. He's got asthma. And Pompey Harbour's bloody freezing this time of year, and the tide runs like a bastard. If he goes down, he won't come up again. And that's a fact.'

The level of condescension a man like Nick Elliott could deploy was inbred through generations. The contempt he displayed could strip off facial skin.

'You are a traitor, sir,' he said. 'You are an absolute disgrace.'

'And Crabb's a sucker,' Knowles replied. 'He's an

honest Englishman, and he thinks that men like you are too. You're not, though, are you? Men like you are bastards. You do not give a shining shit.'

Knowles had arranged the meeting himself, through Marion, and had chosen the venue. She had tried to make him come into the office, but he'd said no deal – it was a pub of his own choosing, or nowhere. They were back in the Tipperary, in a corner, but well visible to the crowd. Knowles did not trust this man an inch.

But in his own eyes, Elliott was the consummate professional. He contemplated bawling out the man in overalls in front of him, reducing him to a jelly of humiliation with the guns of class and privilege. He could break him in so many, many ways.

He chose dismissiveness. He cocked his head, tossed off his whisky – no beer for him today; they were beyond that phase – and merely smiled.

'Worse than a traitor, you are a fool,' he said. 'Whatever you think about it, Crabb will do this job for me, and Crabb will triumph. You, I fear, are rather cowardly. Contemptible. You fill me with contempt.'

Syd Knowles was not contemptible, and well he knew it. He almost broke the rigid face in front of him with the warmth of his own smile.

'If you say so, cocker,' he said, gaily. 'I've spouted all I came to say. Give my regards to Sir Anthony, won't you? And tell him you're a bloody liar.'

He merged into the crowd of inkies and dispatch men so fast and subtly that Elliott was marooned. He knocked over his whisky glass while trying to place it on the little table, and left in some disorder. They were mocking him.

Eleven

Sydney, in his fight to save Crabb's life, turned next to MI5, where he had contacts who 'weren't such a bunch of stuck-up wankers.' Like MI6 they weren't exactly normal men, but most of them had been in the services, and some had come up through the ranks.

'Some of them,' he'd told his wife once, 'have even got some actual brains.'

They were quite cagey, though, and they gave him an earful when he'd made his pitch. He didn't exactly say that Crabb was planning a defection, but he said he'd been invited to some parties, *by* some parties, that Syd thought might be 'on the edge.' When he dropped in the words 'Queen Mother,' he picked up the flicker from three pairs of eyes. He'd hit the spot.

If anyone could stop it, these men could. The die was cast.

Elliott meanwhile, with no inkling that this was happening, signed off a memo denigrating Sydney in the harshest language, and suggesting 'sanctions' be considered. Knowles had come up with an address – he knew he could not avoid it, finally – and a 'more loyal pair of operatives' were sent to speak to Buster Crabb, and set up a tryst.

Bribed with Grant's and Navy Cut – Marion Wilson's input – Crabb arrived at the chosen hotel dressed almost normally, apart maybe from the glittering monocle and the pork pie hat. Elliott eyed up his beige tweeds with feigned admiration while Crabb twirled his cane.

'Buster! My dear chap, how very good to see you after all this time!'

Marion's 'garden gnome' had been delivered smoothly to the private alcove – already wired-up by the microphone brigade – and Elliott clasped his hand.

'Champagne!' he said. 'I've ordered champagne naturally, but I expect you'd like a drop of the hard stuff first, if I know my man? Do you remember that time in Tobermory? When you helped us out with that chap...gosh, who was it now? That bloody kilt! Good God, I ought – oh, to hell with it!'

Elliott was the product of an upbringing so rarefied that he was certain class was basically a nonsense. If a chap was proper he'd get on with another proper chap, and that was that. Although Syd Knowles had shaken this conviction a wee bit, Crabb proved the rule. Despite his memory of the truth, he was grinning ear-to-ear. The Tobermory galleon! What a summer that had been. Although they hadn't—

'Duke of Argyll, sir! That was him! Although I don't—'

I don't recall that you were there, he'd been going to say, but Elliott did not give him the chance.

'Argyll! Indeed it was! With that whore of a Duchess of his! And what about that drunken Saturday in the Mishnish! They had to carry us back to the boat, as I remember, you and me both. Fine example to the Bible bashers, what? The Wee Free, they call themselves up there, you know? One-way ticket to hell in a handcart.'

Crabb was not above a bit of social climbing, so in half an hour they were bosom friends again. As Crabbie told another new best friend – the barman – later, 'I'd have kissed his arse to get this diving job. The daft twat thought he spoke our language. He thought that we were brothers of the soul!'

Brothers or not, Elliott embarked on a potted retelling of Crabb's diving life so full of admiration it might have made another man suspicious. But two large Grant's had started off the action, and champagne flowed like water. The Robber Barons used alcohol as a fuel and a way of life, and the Cold War, when it started, had been custom-made for them. The vodka-sodden ranks of the KGB were much nearer to their equals than any Nazi spy had ever been.

'It's extraordinary, your natural brilliance,' said Elliott. 'Your father was a commercial traveller, I believe, and your mother a humble Streatham housewife. But you became the greatest diver that the world has ever known.'

'Flattery, sir, flattery. I like it! And anyone who calls my old ma humble never met the old bitch, eh?'

Class again. A joke? Elliott gave a nervous guffaw.

'Bitch, eh? Well, Lionel! I certainly would not dare to call my mater that! My mother, that is. My ... er ... my old ma. But please, call me Nick, not sir. I hope that you'll agree to work for us. Not in the services, now, are we? All behind us, those dreadful times.'

'Dreadful were they, sir? Sorry, I mean Nick, that is. Quite honestly, mate, sometimes I wish they'd never fucking ended. Oh, pardon my French. Is it all right to call you mate?'

Elliott drained the bottle into the frogman's glass. Out of nowhere a flunkey appeared with another one, and eased the cork out with the smallest hiss. The bubbles rose.

'Of course it is!'

'And my friends give me Crabbie, mainly. I can't imagine why!'

'Not Buster, then? That's what most people seem to call you.'

Crabb hiccupped. His eyes were no longer quite so bright. His pork pie hat, which had been on the table beside his left hand, was suddenly on the floor. As he leaned over to retrieve it, another flunkey materialised and beat him to it, just avoiding cracking heads.

'Nah,' he said. 'That's a sort of joke, to be quite honest. That Yankee film star, you know, played Flash Gordon, he was Buster Crabbe with an "e" on it in the thirties. He was a gold medal swimmer – and I am bloody not! Without the flippers on I can't hardly do a length, in actual fact. He was a pin-up too, but no one ever said I was, and that's a bleeding fact.'

'You're too modest. For my money, as well as being a human being of the highest possible integrity, you are undoubtedly the best frogman England's ever had, and probably the best one in the world. And that's without a word of flattery.'

Crabb was embarrassed.

'Well, if you say so, sir. Well I did my bit in wartime fair enough, but—'

Elliott interrupted.

'Not just wartime, though. No one speaks more highly of you than my dear friend Jimmy Hedges for example.' He crossed his fingers in the air. 'You were *that* close!'

'HMS *Truculent*,' said Crabb. 'God that was a filthy dive. Hodges by the way, not
Hedges. Jimmy Hodges.'

'Of course, my dear pal Jimmy Hodges. Then all

that hush-hush stuff in Suez.

Wonderful.'

Crabb was nodding, lost in memories. He could taste and feel the brackish, blinding, sandy waters of the canal; heavy fuel oil, rotting flesh, the taste of raki that so often saved his life. And then the Tobermory galleon; the cold, clear, cleansing Scottish sea. 'So what went wrong I wonder?' he said quietly. 'Two years ago I was in Portsmouth, commander in the Special Branch, all the booze and women I could handle, then on the scrapheap like a piece of shit. What a way to treat a fucking hero.' Elliott's face was a portrait of concern.

'It's a failing of this country, I'm afraid,' he said. 'I don't know why your face stopped fitting, Crabbie, but it surely did. It's disgusting, shameful. And you miss the old life, do you?'

'You're joking, sir, you bet I fucking do! What is there that matches up to war? Even to a bloody Cold War. Sometimes I think I'm going to die of boredom.'

Elliott was nodding. His face was serious. Judicious.

'And we can't have that, now can we? It's such a waste, a waste.' He paused. 'Whatever your supposed friend Sydney Knowles might say. I—'

'Syd? What's that? Has he been—'

'No listen, don't mind that, Buster. Look, I've got a proposition for you. Not unofficial or official, but...

Well look, I can't promise you your job back in the Navy, not yet at any rate, but there'll be a fair amount of money for you, cash in hand. And a great deal more in... well, let's call it kudos.'

'Christ,' said Crabb. 'Jesus.' His voice grew stronger. 'But Syd, though? Just what shit did Knowlesy say?'

Elliott turned his head on one side.

'Not shit, exactly,' he said. 'And I think it showed a genuine concern for you. Syd said it was far too cold to dive in Portsmouth Harbour this time of year, and you wouldn't do it in a month of Sundays – you'd run a mile.'

'What, because I'm yellow?! The fucking toe-rag! I'll—'

'No, no, no, no!' said Elliott. 'No Lionel, please don't get me wrong! He was concerned for you! We all are! Crabbie, if you have any doubts at all, if you have the slightest, tiniest hint of fear—'

'Fear! *Fear*! So help me God I'll fucking kill the fucking bastard! I'll—' He stopped. He stared at Elliott's face. Which was filled with sympathy. Concern.

'But why?' he said. 'For fuck sake, Syd and me have... Why?'

Nick Elliott was nodding, as if struggling for understanding. His words came out half as a question.

'Because you were too old? That's what Sydney seemed to be saying. He said—' And then a decision had been made. The bland face hardened, and cleared. The gleam of truth and frankness lit up those honest, Eton eyes.

'Oh, to hell with it,' said Elliott. 'He said you wouldn't even dip a bleeding toe in, and bollocks to your King and country, because you weren't fit enough and you damn well knew it. That's what your dear friend Syd said, and in those very words. And quite frankly, Commander Crabb – if it's true – I'll back him all the way. I will not let you do the dive. I will forbid it!'

As Elliott held his breath, Crabb's eyes – tired and a little bloodshot – slowly filled with tears. His monocle slipped down on to his cheek.

'Oh God, sir!' His voice was shaky. 'Oh God, sir, please tell me that you're not serious. Oh God, there's nothing in this life I'd rather do than do that dive, sir. I've got to do it. I've *got* to.'

'But are you fit, Lionel? You must tell me honestly. Are you fighting fit?'

He raised a finger to the hoverers on the fringe. A man in morning coat stepped towards the table.

'Of course I'm fit,' said Buster Crabb. 'I'm fitter than a butcher's fucking dog! Centum per fucking cent. And when I've done the job, Syd Knowles fucking dies!'

Nick Elliott smiled.

'I think we'll have some brandy, please,' he told the footman. 'Lionel, my dear chap, is there any single marque that you prefer?'

Crabb was blinking. He pulled up his monocle and wiped it clumsily. He cleared phlegm from his throat.

'So long it's wet and makes you fall down pissed,' he started. Then coughed phlegm again. 'I couldn't give a tinker's toss.' He shook his head, and rammed the monocle back in his eye socket. His cough became a liquid rattle, which soon became a laugh.

'Just bring it on!" he said. 'Bring it on and fuck that bastard Knowles to buggery. Hey – what a fucking toe-rag, eh?'

Twelve

Whether or not Anthony Eden did have 'a pair of bollocks in those fancy trews,' he did get wind of the machinations about the Russian visit, as Sydney Knowles intended. The tip-off came from MI5, as part of the never-ending struggle between the two departments. Had anybody dared to tell him of this mutual hatred, the Prime Minister would have been appalled. He was a gentleman. He believed that people worked together for the common good.

To achieve a visit from Khrushchev and Bulganin at this stage of the post-war freeze he considered as perhaps his greatest triumph, and he'd clinched the final details some months before. Cold War was not a phrase he cared to use – his favoured terms were 'limited conflict' or 'competitive co-existence' – and many thought he was at heart a pacifist.

The fact was, that while most politicians professed to believe in John von Neumann's MAD theory – mutually assured destruction – many of them skated very close to 'giving it a try'. Eden was not one of them. He realised that the next war would be possibly the last.

Back in September, when the visit was being finalised, Sir John Sinclair, boss of MI6, had allowed himself to crow at the possibilities it presented. Indeed, he had been almost frothing at the mouth.

'Good heavens, sir. That is a triumph. It's the opportunity we've been waiting on for years! Unprecedented!'

'Opportunity?' Sir Anthony said frostily. 'Opportunity to do what, pray?'

'Well, sir…' Sinclair knew his man, and knew he had spoken prematurely. But surely this milk-and-water apology for a leader was not planning to forego such a golden chance?

'Well?' the PM said.

Sir John harrumphed.

'I might merely point out, sir, that when we had our Royal Navy ships in

Vladivostok some months ago the water round them was positively black with Russian divers. They were like swarms of tadpoles.'

'Your point being…?'

This was ridiculous. Sinclair blinked.

'I might also add, sir, we did send divers down when the *Sverdlov* was here last summer. At the specific and urgent request of Navy Intelligence. No repercussions, sir. None at all.'

'And no result – or am I wrong on that? The report that crossed my desk said our two frogmen may have discovered an underwater recess in the hull. I emphasise the word *may*. It was a failure.'

A brief stand-off. Then Sinclair said: 'There will be three ships this time. With Khrushchev and Bulganin on board. Important men, sir. Defended with the very latest in technology. At the very least, their underwater profiles—'

Eden cut him off.

'With respect, this is not a job for buccaneers.' His voice grew colder. 'This is a matter of the most crucial diplomacy in international affairs since the war. We will take no action of any sort that carries the slightest risk of upsetting that. Is this understood?'

Sinclair had to respond. It was the protocol. But not necessarily with the absolute truth.

'If I may say so, I fear you might have slightly misunderstood my drift, sir. Of course there will be no such operation. It is not my intention, and it never was. I trust we can agree on that.'

Beneath the neat moustache, a slight curling of the PM's upper lip was just discernible.

'They are our guests, Sinclair. However you think the Russians might behave, we will not sink to their level. We are not peasants. The potatoes that we grow in this country are for eating, not distilling into third-rate hooch. We are not vodka-raddled thugs.'

On that level, at least, they understood each other. But there were other ways to get around it. Sinclair's men were Robber Barons. They had their methods and their means.

Thirteen

Syd Knowles tracked down Crabbie one last time because – whatever shit it took – he was going to save him from himself. But when he found him, in a seedy little Soho club, he figured that he might have come too late. He did not know that Elliott had stabbed him in the back.

It was not off his own bat entirely, in any case, this visit. Pat Rose, who had a growing sense that things were coming to a head, had rung him up in Lancashire again. She did not know it was a diving job – Lionel denied that, drunk or sober – but she had a deep-down fear. She hoped for reassurance.

'It's kicking off,' she said. 'I know it is, Syd, something's happening. He's like a cat on coals. There's been phone calls and he's drinking like there's no tomorrow. Can you come down, love? Down to London? I need to talk, love. Please.'

'I've already spoke to him,' said Syd. 'I've told him any scheme he hears is crazy, I've told him to ignore it, however sweet the offer is. I think he'll... Between you and me, Pat, I've slipped him a few quid.'

'Oh, right,' she said. She caught her breath; her

voice was bitter. 'That's where he's got the extra from then, is it? His flat's knee-deep in whisky bottles now, so thanks a lot, love. Thanks a ruddy bunch.'

Syd bit his lip. He'd opened up the whisky tap, but he'd hoped it might make Crabb too pissed to bother diving. Which was a prattish thing to think, prattish. He'd have to try again; try harder.

Pat was struggling with her anger.

'Sometimes you worry me,' she said. 'Sometimes I think you're as daft as bloody he is. But I need to talk, I've got to. Can you come down to London? Can Joan? Please, Syd. Please.'

He could. He had to.

'I can. I bloody will,' he said. 'Listen, I'm hauling paper down to Fleet Street in a day or so, so I'll get across to see you, definite. Aw reet?'

'It's not that I don't love him, Syd, because I do, you know that, don't you? It's just that he's a—'

'I know that too, love. He is. He's doesn't know he's bloody born.'

Pat got her wits together, suddenly.

'What crazy scheme?' she said. 'What offer? It's not another bloody diving job they're trying to make him do, is it? He swears black and white he... I'm right though, aren't I? I'm right! Syd, he's not capable! It'll kill him! Syd!'

'No,' lied Knowles. 'Not diving, Pat, he's not as daft as that. It's... Look, I'll come and see you. Then

I'll go and bollock him again. Don't give up hope, love, it's not that bloody bad, is it? I doubt if there's anything... Look, it'll just be some scheme to make some money.'

He felt a lying bastard and a fool. And he felt determination growing in his stomach. He had no actual need to go to London at the moment, not for a week or so in fact. But he packed his bag next morning, early, and fired up his ERF. It had a Gardner 180, the greatest diesel engine in the world. Before long he was eating up the miles.

The club where he found Crabb was quite unpleasant, infested with the sort of tarts that brought Syd out in spots. But when he saw his target in the noisy gloom – his friend, his diving mucker of three war zones and half a dozen countries – his heart sank further. He crossed the room in ten paces, took the whisky out of Crabbie's hand, and said full in his face: 'Don't do it, mate. For fuck's sake stop. Don't fucking do it.'

As near as damn it, Crabb's eyes swivelled in his head. He was in his most garish suit and the pork pie titfer was at an absurdly rakish angle. Syd had no doubts. Crabb was searching for a woman. Crabb was desperate. Crabb, maybe, was mad.

'Syd, you bastard! What the fuck do you want?'

'Bastard' was an endearment term, and momentarily, Crabb's eyes went steady. Then he remembered. He didn't like Syd now, did he? Syd was a traitor. Endearment was out of the question. Totally.

'You cunt,' he mumbled. 'You fucking twat. What d'you mean I'm fucking past it?' His eyes reverted. What was he on about? What had Sydney done? He had forgotten.

'Where's me Scotch?' he said. 'What you drinking, sunshine? Terence – give this man a whisky. Big one, on the slate. Then ring up that Gaynor and tell her she can screw herself, will you?' He blinked rapidly. The monocle was hanging on its ribbon. 'Where's me eye-piece? What you here for, Sydney? I've been stood up again. Some women just ain't got no bleeding manners.'

Pat was the saddest thing of all for Syd. She'd been with Crabb before he'd married Margaret, even, and when that had gone tits up they'd started up again, the love that wouldn't die, etcetera. The saddest thing of all.

'For God's sake, mate,' he said. 'You've had enough. We'll go back home and drink some coffee. Laurence, call a taxi will you? Smartish.'

'The nearest rank's in Dean Street. Not far to walk,' said the barman. He smiled maliciously. 'It's Terence, by the way. Pat dumped him. It was the booze or her; it was the cards and horses and the dirty ten-bob tarts. I'm quoting.' The smile got broader. 'It's not a secret, pal. He tells me everything does Crabbie. I'm his best mate. Ask him.'

'Crabb!' snapped Sydney. 'I'm not going to ask you anything, I'm *telling* you. You – Terence, Laurence, Mr Pissing Magoo! – piss off out of earshot before I break your pissing neck. Crabbie, fucking listen!'

It was ten minutes before he got any sense out of him, by which time Syd was drained, almost past caring. They got a cab in Dean Street, and he half-dragged him upstairs to his dirty little room. Crabb was a salesman now, the mighty fallen just about as low as one could fall, and it hurt Syd to the bone. He made him tea, and laid him on his bed, and tried again to talk some sense to him.

'You're old,' he said. 'You're nearly fifty. You've got a drink problem that you could walk a dog on, you wheeze like an asthmatic bloodhound. This job, Crabbie, is going to kill you. You are not to do it. You are not fucking going to do it. Listen to me. I am your friend.'

Crabb argued, slept, woke, listened more, then argued. The upshot was, he said, that he was doing it. Nick Elliott wanted him, his country wanted him, there was no other bugger living who could hope to bring it off. Syd was jealous. Syd was a prat. Syd was a traitor and an arsehole. And there was nothing Syd could say that would make a tiny bit of difference, nothing in the world.

So Syd prepared to fire his bazooka.

'I told them,' he said. 'Listen Crabbie, I went along to MI5, and I bloody told them. That bastard Elliott don't give a flying fart about you or me, he don't care if we live or fucking die. So I said I wouldn't do it, and you wouldn't neither. Neither of us. We don't go near no Russkie warships. Never.'

Crabb hoisted himself up onto his elbow, quite indifferent. The bedsprings creaked.

'So you're a prat,' he said. 'And you're a liar, too, because I am going underneath them, ain't I? I'm bored to fucking death, Syd, don't you get that? This is my one last chance to feel that I'm alive. Even if it fucking kills me.'

'It's you who doesn't get it, mate,' Knowles said. 'I went to MI5. I told them you're a Russian spy. I told them you've sold out. I told them that you're going to defect.'

For a long moment, Crabb did not speak. Then he blew breath out through his nostrils, not loudly but to great effect. He almost seemed amused. The big bazooka? More like a damp squib.

'What did you do that for then, Sydney? Are you off your trike? I'd never be a Russian spy. I can't stand the taste of fucking vodka.'

Syd's voice was calm.

'I've heard you talking, haven't I? And you've been to parties, you even dragged me along one time. MI6. That raving poofter Burgess. That long, tall streak of fairy queen called Blunt. And all the other arsehole bandits.'

'Bollocks,' said Crabb. 'If nothing else I'm not a queer, mate, you know that. And they have good parties. And me and Mr Blunt discuss fine art. We do! You just haven't got my class, have you, my little Northern friend? See you in a proper suit! See you with a Spanish fucking swordstick! Get out of here and go and find your clogs!'

Syd rode the insults. He had more shots left in his locker.

'What about that time in Keppel's Head, by Pompey dockyard gates? We were in a mass of Navy officers, and you buttonholed the biggest stuck-up prat of all. The Russians know how to treat a hero, that's what you said; our lot treat us like bleeding scum. We had to rush you across the Gosport ferry before the night-stick boys got called. You was serious. You was on the point of bloody going Commie.'

But Crabb seemed sober now.

'A load of bollocks, chum,' he said. 'Sydney, that is hot cock. If you told that to MI5 you're barking. It's not me who'll get arrested – you'll end up in the loony bin, old son. And I won't bail you out, I promise you.'

Knowles *had* told them that, and God knows in his heart he might have thought it true. Whatever, he thought it would save Crabbie from himself, and that would be enough. Crabb was a hero. He was a hero who did not deserve to die.

'In any case, you cunt, you've missed the boat,' Crabb added. 'They've signed me up already, cash in hand. I'll be in Pompey harbour in a week or two, blowing bubbles like a fucking goldfish – for King and country, like in the good old days. Spying for Russia, my left tit! Now fuck off and let me get some kip. And thank you, Sydney. You've cheered me up no end!'

Fourteen

The hints that got through to Eden did not add up to much, but Sir John Sinclair of MI6, and his fellow brass, were called in for a meeting. The Cabinet Secretary was there, stenographers, the lot. Kim Philby wasn't, naturally; such gatherings were no longer in his purlieu. But strangely, only two days later, he mentioned it to Elliott in their club. And Elliott did not ask him how he knew.

The Prime Minister's purpose was to reiterate the value of the Russian visit to the State. It was not just courtesy, it was of phenomenal importance to the safety – nay survival – of the western world. Any hint to the Soviets that they were being spied upon would be disgusting. What's more it might be fatal. Literally.

Each man in the room in turn was fixed with Eden's less than beady eye. There were no women present, not even taking notes; this was man's work. And finally, after half an hour of reiteration, the PM wound it up.

'Gentlemen, I thank you. And to sum up once more, there will be no surveillance, of any sort, by any agency, of these Russian ships. I have given them my word of honour, which is my bond. What has been said within these walls will stay between these walls. I thank you.'

Among the things he'd promised the Russians, was that any room they might stay in would not be wired for the visit. But as all relevant hotels in the capital were 'bugged to buggery already', as Peter 'Bugger' Lunn told his cohorts, there was no problem in keeping that promise, was there?

'Claridge's has got more copper wires than a submarine's magneto, like all the best hotels,' he lisped. 'The Reds aren't stupid, are they? If they want to keep their secrets secret, they only need to keep their mouths shut. Simple.'

Maybe they were stupid, then. Or maybe rather subtle, with a Slavic sense of mockery. For not long after they'd booked into their wonderful hotels, guaranteed surveillance free, Lunn's operatives were reporting rather funny stories. How Khrushchev, for instance, spent hours before the mirror in his suite discussing his wardrobe with his footman, up to and including the style and tightness of his underpants. He also talked about his haemorrhoids a lot, and what sort of scented ointment would prove enticing to a lady of the night.

'They're so damnably middle class, the Communists,' Elliott told Philby over cocktails. 'So fucking bourgeois. *Vive la revolution!*'

'Or maybe they take the piss,' said Philby, languidly. 'Nikita in his nightie playing ping pong with his piles sounds a bit unlikely. What do they think of it in Navy Int? Does it excite them? Backside rules the Navy, doncher know.'

'Well, my source *is* Ian Fleming, although he's back in civvy street officially. But while he's pretty bent, he's certainly no homosexual. It's whips and rubber suits he drools about. And great big floppy flippers!'

'Droll,' said Kim. 'The most perverted man I've ever met, and they say he wants to get off his so-called thrillers now and write a book for children. Yes, you heard. About a flying car called Chitty Chitty Bang Bang.'

'Chitty Chitty what?!' said Elliott. 'That's not a car, that's what the squaddies stuck out East used to call a weekend pass-out for the knocking shop. Get your chitty, get your bang-bang. Filthy Friday and a dose.'

'I can't say you're wrong, old man,' said Philby, 'but will the pretty little mumsies know? Imagine them reading it aloud to the precious kiddie-winkies. Loins on fire, what? Knees akimbo in the nursery! A whole new meaning to the cloak and dagger.'

Elliott roared with laughter.

'More cloacus and dagging, knowing Fleming though,' he said. 'He likes it very dirty. And a lot!'

'And long,' said Philby. 'A lot and very long. A bit

like Russian literature, in a general way. I wonder what the Reds'll make of Buster Crabb?'

The look on Elliott's face alerted him. Shit! Too much thinking out aloud.

'Just a silly notion,' he went on briskly. 'Some rumour I picked up, you'll tell me it's all nonsense. I was actually thinking of those long, boring books. I mean, I'm not even sure that Buster Crabb can read, are you?'

Elliott raised his glass carefully and took a sip.

'Crabb?' he said. 'Long, boring books? I'm really not sure I know what you're on about. Should I?'

'Well, there you go!' said Kim. 'One stupid rumour scotched. I thought I'd heard some talk that he was turning Commie. I didn't, did I? Must have imagined it.'

'Full marks for speed, at least,' laughed Elliott, relieved. 'It's being put about by MI5, we think, and it's total, utter bullshit. Buster, as you damn well know, is as straight as a die, not a treacherous bone in his whole body. What do you think?'

'I'll raise a glass to that,' said Kim. 'But imagine if some heartless scum should tell the Reds such tosh, though! Truly, traitors are the greatest evil in the world. I'd boil them alive.'

Stupid talk or not though, first thing next morning Elliott sent MI5 a stiff memo ridiculing some hints he believed they'd been disseminating that Crabb had Russian sympathies, and insisting they should cut it out forthwith. He suggested Sydney

Knowles had started the hare running, because the man was jealous of Crabb, and wished to stir things up. He insisted that an official black mark should be attached to his file.

He sent another memo then, through Marion, to a dive master he had used before. He appointed him to keep an eye on Crabb, sort out his money and equipment, see to any refresher training he might wish to undergo, and 'give him the respect due to a man who had saved many lives, and won the George Medal in so doing.' He further warned him that there were 'elements' who might denigrate Crabb's personality – and his sobriety in particular – and that they should be treated with contempt.

The dive master was therefore quite astonished to find Commander Crabb extremely drunk the first time that he met him, and on three more occasions after that. He reported it to an MI6 technical officer called John Henry, who reported up the line. Lionel Crabb, he said, was a heavy drinker, had blood pressure off the scale and was heading for a heart attack.

Elliott's response was brutal and immediate. Both Henry and his informant were relieved of their duties with a reprimand, and from hereon in, a former sailor in the MI6 liaison unit, Ted Davis, would be the only man to handle Buster Crabb.

There would be no more 'knocking talk' about this British hero.

Fifteen

In desperation, when the whole thing seemed to be unstoppable, Syd drove south to see Pat Rose again, and worried her half sick. He told her they had to find Crabbie, to dig him out, to talk to him, to kick some sense into his stupid head.

But time was racing on, and Crabb was playing hard to get – he was as slippery as an eel, said Pat. Syd did manage to bluff his way through to Marion on the phone on one occasion, but that depressed him even worse. It was as if she'd never heard of him – or Crabb, for that matter. Knowles shouted down the phone that she was a heartless bitch.

He did a regular circuit of the clubs seeking him out though, until he had to go back north again. He also hammered at his contacts, and the day he left, a lead came through from Mr Pendock, Crabb's so-called partner.

'He'll be in this drinks dive on the edge of Soho probably tonight,' Pendock told Pat. 'Not as grim as while the war was on, but pretty...you know. Shall I come with you?'

Pat demurred. Low clubs held no fears for her,

and if anyone tried it on, for any reason, she'd hack them with her heels – Crabb included if he played the bloody fool.

But she preferred the ultimate approach. The ultimatum. If he was likely drinking that evening, he'd likely be at his flat that day. She kicked seven bells out of his door to see if he was in, then pushed a big note through his letterbox and told three neighbours to tell him it was there.

It did the trick. Three hours later she got a phone call and she got invited to a club. Pat, dizzy with success that her ploy had worked, almost said yes. Truth was, the sound of his voice, after all her knock-backs and blind allies, flooded her with relief.

'Where've you been, you rotten bastard!' she burst out. 'Lionel, you pig, I've been searching for you! I've been bloody desperate! I thought you might be bloody dead! You shitbag!'

'Wow,' said Buster, calmly. 'Nice to hear from you too, darling! Thanks for the lovely note, an' all – very ladylike. I take it you'll pay me for the new front door?'

'Don't make me laugh, you pig!' she said. She was halfway between tears and giggles now. 'Oh you bastard, Lionel, where *have* you been?'

'You won't believe me, I've been busy. I haven't even had a drink for ages, I'm like a lickle desert flower. There's a place I know. A lovely place. Gin and orange from a fountain. Gin and bitters. Gin and It.'

'Port and lemon, that's what I fancy,' said Pat Rose. She heard the words tumble from her lips. 'No! Lionel, stop it! You can't sweet talk me, you bastard! Where've you *been*?'

'Where are we going, that's the proper question, though. A night of love! Dancing! Music! Booze! And after that – who knows?'

Pat came to her senses.

'Farting in my bed,' she said, 'that's what I know. Last time you took me out you pissed all in my wardrobe, too. No, Lionel – no clubbing. If you want to come, you can come and have some supper. I'd like that, honestly, I'd really, really like that. No clubbing, though. I will not come clubbing.'

'Ah well,' he said. 'Your funeral. I've got some money, Pat, I've got a quid or two. Port and lemon till it comes out of your ear'oles! Or any other orifice you fancy!'

When he got rude it meant his mood was good. Pat tried to feel elated.

'Ooh Lionel, you are a dirty sod. What money, love? Where from? Look, come and have a little bit of supper round my place. Mr Cracknell says he's got some lovely chops. Where've you been?'

She didn't expect a straight answer, she knew her man too well, and she didn't get one. Point was, he told her, he'd have to go off in a day or two, and he'd been dead busy on some… Like, well, pretty important stuff. Hush-hush. Diving? Diving? What was she on about? Why was she so obsessed?

Inwardly, Pat sighed. It was typical, she thought; the business was so hush-hush he just *had* to mention it, but if she wanted details, she could sing for them. He was stringing her along again. And in a day or two he'd bugger off. It was time she called a halt. It was time to get it on the line. Commitment. A vision of a bleeding future.

Then she felt better. He said he wanted to see her anyway, he'd missed her. Soft Pat just melted, as he had guessed she would. He'd thought it was time they had a big night out, he wheedled; but even better – a long night in.

Crabb did not say – and he didn't say it later – that he'd been involved in several emergency sessions with top medicos, including trips to Haslar Hospital to see the diving experts. As well as getting fitted for the latest two-piece rubber suit, which also took a damned long time.

All that he'd tell her later, if at all. For now, a night in bed would be enough. He really loved her, really, old Pat Rose. He really did.

Sixteen

The emergency sessions, in London and then in the diving complex, had come about because Ted Davis, of MI6 liaison, had added his two penn'orth to the health-and-fitness worries.

John Henry and Syd Knowles had suffered for their frankness, but Davis – 'very good man; very, very sound' – had gone so far as to wonder formally about the consequences if Crabb did not survive. Unlike the 'amateurs' he had gone through the proper channels, so Nick Elliott could not ignore it. But still he did not like the interference.

'Survive?' he snapped. 'Good God, what utter steaming balls is this?'

The woman he was shouting at was Marion, and he instantly regretted it. 'Don't shoot the messenger' had always been his watchword, and this messenger had brought it to his attention with her usual quiet charm.

'My dear,' he said. 'That was unconscionable. I am a beast.'

'The steaming balls,' said Marion levelly, 'is apparently a genuine concern. Mr Crabb is drinking like a fish, according to Davis. He is on a hundred cigarettes a day, and lives on cake and Guinness. Guinness may indeed be good for you, sir, but not that good.' A small smile lit her lips. 'I'm not a doctor, though.'

He held his temples in his palms.

'Fuck!' he said. 'And when's the bastard due to dive?'

It sounds like 'die,' thought Marion.

'Not until the nineteenth, sir,' she said. 'Commander Crabb is due at *Vernon* for fitting and equipment briefings before then. Should I arrange for medical assessments too? All the experts work from there.'

Nick Elliott thought hard. There were experts and experts, obviously. He examined Marion's face. Calm, and bright. And possibly, he hoped, adoring.

'Hmm,' he said. 'No time for overkill, is there? Perhaps a general check would be the best. Some of these medicos get over-precious sometimes. Anxious to prove a point, know what I mean? They may not have the least conception of how vitally important this little jaunt might prove to be.'

Marion was smiling. Yes, thought Elliott, adoring.

'It's just a little swim for Buster Crabb,' she said. 'I've been reading him up. You were right, sir, I had completely underestimated him. An amazing man. Extraordinary heroism. I'm sure he'd hate it if he didn't get to dive.'

This time he looked at her so hard he caused a blush to rise.

'I'll leave it up to you, my dear,' he said. 'Marion, I can't say how glad I am to have you on side. If you sort this for me, I will be eternally grateful. You are indeed a poppet.'

When Elliott called in Crabb to meet him at another of his small, discreetly bugged hotels, he dubbed it jokily 'one last face-to-face.' He did not offer champagne this time, but Guinness. Crabbie raised an eyebrow.

'Never touch the stuff,' he said. 'You've been misinformed. It's a drink for Fenians from the bog. I wouldn't mind a Jameson's, though. To show I'm not a racist.'

'I had to laugh,' Nick told Philby in the grandees' later. 'He's a gutsy little bastard, no getting away from that. I came straight out with it: told him I'd had some negatives about his health…if he was well enough to do the job. I didn't want him bobbing up and down in Portsmouth Harbour like a busted tractor tyre!'

'How did he react?'

'Fair play old boy, he took it rather well. Said he expected it came from John Henry or maybe Davis, and Henry was a twat who'd always been jealous of his reputation. He was kinder about Ted Davis; said he was a nice lad, but sentimental.'

'Ah.'

'The upshot was he told me they were barking; he got quite passionate. He'd never been what you'd call fighting fit by some people's yardsticks, and he'd saved more tonnage than any other frogman you could name. Then he said he'd go down on his knees and beg me if that's what it took to get the job, but he didn't think I was that sort of a wanker. He can be extremely funny when he wants to. He was laughing at me.'

'He's not a coward, then. He must know that you could block him with a finger-click.'

'He's extremely not a coward, not in any way. In my opinion he's as tough as wire rope. Men like Buster Crabb, Kim, are damn near indestructible.'

He paused. He sipped his drink. He laughed.

'We'll find out soon enough, in any case. The Russians are due in on the eighteenth and I'm sending Buster down by train the day before. Sally Port Hotel on High Street, opposite Portsmouth Cathedral. Close enough for one last pray if that's what he fancies.'

'You are so cynical, Nicholas. Is he taking a big team?'

'Nah. Just one or two. That CIA man, do you remember him? Smith. He doesn't give a good goddam, they say.'

'He doesn't what?'

'A joke. What the Yanks take for a witticism. It's what they call him: Goddam Smith. They put Coca Cola in their whisky, too. And they think they're civilized.'

Later that night in England, the early hours of the morning Moscow time, an agent codenamed Peach sent an encrypted message to his KGB controller, which was relayed to the cruiser *Ordzhonikidze*. She was in the North Atlantic with two destroyer escorts, heading for the British Isles.

Ultimately, their destination was Portsmouth Harbour. The captain, commissar and KGB co-ordinator began to plan.

They were looking forward to a meeting with Commander Crabb.

Seventeen

Mr Cracknell, it seemed, had sold Pat's chops to another hungry housewife, but he offered her 'a lovely little bit of roasting beef.' She'd also got some good coal in - not the smokeless crap that they were pushing now - so for a celebration dinner, everything was looking good.

She was a good cook and although it was mid-April London was still chilly, so she got the fire blazing up the chimney. When Crabb arrived the dinner was well on and for once he did not want a drink. When she teased him about it, he confessed that the job he had to go on was next day.

'So what sort of job?' she asked. She tried to keep it very light. 'You sell cheap furniture, Lionel. What you going to do, set up a branch in Oxford Street?'

The joke passed him by. He seemed on edge.

'Oxford Street? What's that got to do with it?'

She tried again.

'You're nervous, love. What's going on? Look tell me, Lionel. Please. It's not another diving thing, is it?'

He rolled his eyes, but Pat persisted. At last he opened up a bit, but he only told a partial truth. He admitted that he had to go to Pompey to test some gear. There would be diving, maybe, but not serious – they thought he was too old to do a proper job. So even if he'd wanted to he had no chance. He was past it!

'What do they know about diving?' he said. 'They know bugger all.'

That was meant to be a joke, but it came out false as hell. Pat grunted.

'Well I s'pose they think they know this much, pet,' she said, carefully. 'Portsmouth Harbour's got a tide that runs like stink, you've often said so. You hate the ruddy place. And anyway—'

She stopped, and eyed him quizzically.

'Hang on,' she went on. 'Tomorrow, did you say? So when are those Russkie ships due in? It's in the papers. They were talking about it in the butcher's. Oh Lionel, you're not spying on the bloody Commies are you?'

Crabb laughed mightily.

'Shut up gal, of course I'm not, you're talking bloody daft. I told you. It's equipment testing. I'll actually be in Stokes Bay, just down past Haslar wall, the other side of Gosport. You do talk bollocks sometimes.'

But she could nag as well as talking bollocks, and nag she did, and nag and nag and nag. Pat had one trump card, because Crabb was a lonely man and they'd been engaged for yonks, and he was getting desperate. Pat could cook. Her flat was nice, unlike his filthy slum-hole. And since she owned it, no one could ever kick her out.

She was also comfortable in bed, as he hoped to reconfirm not too much later. Another reason for laying off the hooch.

Finally he had to do a deal with her, because Pat Rose could outmanoeuvre better men than he was. She persuaded him he wanted her to come down to Portsmouth with him, and persuaded him that he'd persuaded her.

Then, when he had agreed to it, she told him that she wouldn't after all, that he would have to go alone unless... Unless what?

'You've got to tell me why you're going, love. I worry for you, Lionel. And I—'

'But I—'

By this time, against all intentions, Lionel Crabb was tipsy. The Grant's had come out at the chosen moment – timing is everything – and he could not resist a drop of Grant's. Pat's terms were harsh and starkly stated. Tell her everything, or the engagement would be off. Was off. No argument.

'How can I marry a man who doesn't trust me, Lionel? I'm worried for you, love. I want to help you. Please. Don't be too difficult. You love me, don't you?'

The taste and smell of beef was wonderful. The Grant's was mother's milk to him. Good God, he thought, I bloody do an' all. I really think I bloody do.

He stayed awake for nearly half an hour when they went to bed. It was a peaceful night and Pat lay and listened to the streets of London till early morning in a great content. She had a future with him, she was sure of it. Lionel was a lovely, kindly man. A gentleman.

* * *

On the *Ordzhonikidze*, approaching from the north and west, they talked about this little frogman who was a sort of giant of his trade. The men who'd handle him (if he should be taken) and the commissar, were invited to the stateroom to drink vodka with the high and mighty of the land. Comrade Khrushchev, Comrade Bulganin: they did not come higher up the scale than that. Great vodka men, however, who loved to laugh and shout.

'You say he's small,' Nikita asked. 'How big is small?'

'Small enough to crawl up a cruiser's arse-pipe!' boomed Bulganin. 'We'll get a dose of Crabb's they say! Think of it!'

The commissar understood the English slang,

but was a man of deep dishumour. It was a job description, almost.

'*Nyet, nyet,*' he said. 'This is important, Comrade Party Leader. If we can catch him, we can take him home with us. For our Navy, it could be of the deepest seriousness.'

Nikita Khrushchev's waxen jowls shook.

'Indeed!' he shouted. 'Serious indeed! The whole damn Navy will be crawling with Bulganin's lice!'

The commissar did not raise a smile.

Eighteen

By the time their train slowed down for Petersfield on Tuesday evening, Pat Rose had wheedled more State secrets from her man. The name – roughly – of the cruiser he was going to look at, although neither of them could pronounce or spell it, and the name of the man that he'd be diving with.

Also the name of the hotel where they would be staying. Crabb had been most reluctant coming out with this. As if he didn't want her to have the information.

'The Sally Port?' said Pat, when she'd wormed it out at last. 'That's a weird one. Who's she when she's out? Sally in our Alley? What will our room be like?'

'The Sallyport,' said Buster. 'Nothing to do with Sally. It's the gate in the sea wall where sailors sallied out of in the olden days to join ships anchored in Spithead. People like Nelson. He may've stayed there for all I know. I bet he had a better room than I will, though.'

'You will? We will, don't you mean? Or am I sleeping in the garden shed?'

So came the little bombshell. Whatever Crabbie's

room was like they couldn't stay together, of course they couldn't.

'Of course?' she said. 'Of course? What do you bloody think you mean of course? We're getting married! We're engaged! What in the name of goblins do you bloody mean?'

Crabb had chosen a crowded compartment just in case this sort of thing should happen. Pat was inhibited, surely – but not inhibited enough. She appealed to the other passengers, feeding her anger on their embarrassment.

'This man's my bloody husband, nearly! We've been engaged for years! And now he's—'

The train was squeaking into Petersfield. Because God hated her, the other passengers – quite noisily – got off. Lionel tried to make her laugh at that, and failed. Pat's face was like a rat-trap.

'Well?' she said.

'Because I've got to share,' he said. 'Not with another bloody woman, if you're going to be ridiculous, because I'm here to work. I'll be sharing with a man you've met, in actual fact, a man you know. A man called Bernard Smith.'

He could say it now; they were on their own. The wheels slipped as the train accelerated, and the burst of chuffing sounded like ironic laughter.

'And Bernard Smith is? I've never heard the bloody name.'

'He's sort of secret service. He's...well, CIA.'

'CIA?' she said. 'You mean that bloody Yank? That's not Bernard Smith, it's

Matthew, isn't it, you lying bastard! That bloody scum who calls himself "Goddam"?' Crabb, eyes down, lit a Player's with a shaking hand. He drew in smoke, and coughed his lungs up. When he could speak again, Pat was, perhaps, resigned. He was a liar and she'd always known it. Part of his job. What was the bloody point in arguing?

He smiled at her. Tentative. The famous little boy look.

'It's not Goddam, I promise you, it's some US Navy man. But you do remember

Johnny Hobbs in any case, don't you? Blond curly hair, married to that fat girl, Erica? He's a mate of Mr P, my boss. My partner. They live in Havant by the Robin Hood and we're going to have a drink with them, and then they're going to put you up.'

She was interested. This didn't sound too bad. The train had settled down, the scenery was nice.

'When we get to Pompey I'll put you on another train, this one doesn't stop at Havant. Then when I've sorted out me little bits of business, I'll come on up myself. You know Johnny and Erica, they can't hardly wait to see you. Bloody lovely, it'll be.'

Pat didn't put a bet on it but she'd decided not to care, it was too tiring. If he was meeting a Navy man in Pompey, he wouldn't be meeting her in Havant, would he? It stood to reason.

But she decided, for the moment, that it wouldn't bother her. When he waved her off from Portsmouth Harbour station on a stopping train some ninety minutes later, she kissed him carelessly, and told him she did not expect him to turn up that night.

Crabb was aggrieved, which made her feel a great deal better. She kissed him again, much harder, and told him he wouldn't know what he was missing if he didn't make it.

'Don't turn up, and it's your lookout,' she said again, as the engine began to push out smoke and steam explosively. 'If you'd rather get off with a mermaid, that's your decision, Lionel. Depends what you're after love: A bit of meat – or fish!'

Nineteen

As the train dragged off up the line towards Fratton, a man who had been watching them stepped from the shadows. Their fond farewells had filled him with amusement, but affection, too. Crabb was such a funny little bugger, thought Goddam Smith, and it was such a funny little scene. A sort of dwarf dressed to the nines, alongside a comfy lady who could have been his auntie or his wife. And in a couple of hours, the funny little bugger would be deep in cold, black water.

By the time Pat's train had disappeared, though, they had cut through the preliminaries and agreed that it was more than time to have a drink. They'd worked before together. They were comfortable. They appreciated liquor almost equally. Almost.

'So what's the plan?' said Crabbie. 'I don't see no Russkie ships, I thought they were mooring at South Railway slip. Where are the bastards, then?'

The end of the London main line was about three hundred yards from South Railway jetty, and there was clearly nothing moored against it yet. The wind was brisk and chilly, the surface choppy. Very uninviting, Crabbie thought. I bet it's colder than a witch's tit.

Goddam was laughing at him.

'Don't they tell you Limey bastards nothing, mister? Or is it in one ear and gone again? It's tomorrow that they're coming. Three of them, one big cruiser, two lean and hungry timber wolves. Next you'll be saying you don't even know their bloody names!'

'Piss off,' said Crabb. 'It's Khrushchev Tub-o-lard, and Buggery Bulganin.'

'And the ships?'

'Queen Mary, Queen Elizabeth and the Victory, to name but five. Come on,

Smithie, who gives a good goddam! Tomorrow's good. Today we have a little drink or two. Where are they now, though?'

'I'm Goddam Smith, not Gypsy Petrulengo. Out in the Channel someplace, I guess, maybe the Atlantic. Two thousand Ivans supping vodka and dreaming of poxy

Pompey pussy. Christ, who'd be a Russian sailorman? Even their cigarettes are made of cardboard.'

Crabb laughed. He'd known some Russian matelots in his time, when Joe Stalin was a hero, before the bastards rung the Iron Curtain down. They were jolly chaps, most of them. And savage piss artists to a man. World class.

'So if we've got no ships to mine till morning, what's our plan tonight? You take me to the Sally Port Hotel, we drop our gear off, and then what? I've got a date tonight in Havant. Little dump about eight miles from here I used to work in, but it's got a lovely pub. We could go there. Also some friends, a big soft bed and my toasty tart tucked up in it.'

'Paradise on a bun,' said Goddam, drily. 'Well, there's nix to stop you, chum, except we're on official business, so you can count me out. And there might be the question of a drink or two if we stay in town.'

'Hah, now you're talking, brother. And we're travellers, so there's certain laws that don't apply, whatever time of day it is. Even in this daft country you can get a drink in your own hotel. Anyway, I've got a bottle in me baggage. Grant's, naturally.'

Goddam made a face. Satirical.

'No bourbon, then? I call that goddam unfriendly. Come on, let's go. Cab rank's just down there.'

'It's not that far, we can hoof it. Oh, sorry, I forgot. You fucking idle Yankees. But you can pay the fare, okay? I won't get the moolah for this job until it's finished. Come on Russkie cruisers! Time you cruised home to Crabbie...pronto.'

After a few drinks in the Sally Port they had a few drinks more, then – on the insistence of the manager – they signed the register.

'Look,' he said, 'you know the rules, gents. If you're not signed in I can't really serve you legally. I know you've had a few already, but I can't serve you more. Honestly. Play the game, okay? Please?'

Playing games was what Crabb loved, so they both signed in with their real names. Or he did, anyway. How could anyone be sure that Smith was really Smith – he was an MI6 man to his very roots. Or maybe CIA.

'Are you one of ours?' Crabb wondered out aloud, 'or one of Angleton's? Do you love Jesus? James Jesus that is, naturally. Or on the other hand, who bleeding cares?'

Later in the evening, as more men came and more drink flowed, the questions of identity became more shadowy, especially to Buster Crabb. One man he knew was definitely MI6, Ted Davis, moved in and out of the crowded bar, but seemed to be avoiding him – which was not difficult. Although, thought Crabbie, half-cut, isn't he my official handler?

Then later he was led out to a telephone in the lobby, and had a garbled conversation with a Navy officer from *Vernon* who offered 'unofficial help, whatever help was needed,' although Crabb did not know the man from Adam. Then a policeman was introduced, a superintendent called Jack Lamport, and a man in civvies who volunteered to be his dresser and attendant on the dive tomorrow morning

– which Crabb denied with utter vehemence was going to take place.

He caught up with Goddam five minutes afterwards and gabbled, full of drunken panic, that their cover had been broken and everybody in the world knew of the venture. Goddam Smith just laughed at him and clapped him on the back in a way that nearly knocked his lungs out through his ribs.

'Oh Buster, Buster – who gives a good goddam, who gives a flying fuck? Come over here, I've found some bourbon. I'm going to teach you what tough guys really drink! God bless Jack Daniels and America!'

The party finished late, and Lionel Crabb did not get out of town to see his love as promised. He went to bed blinded by drink, and had a bad night, plagued by his usual vicious dreams. The sea played a big part in his nightmares, it flowed into his head, a black and liquid horror. It terrified him.

From Pat Rose's point of view, he missed a damned good night. She and her two friends laughed and drank themselves into euphoria in the Robin Hood, by Havant's little church, and sang till they were hoarse. She got a bit twitchy at closing time, though, and was almost tearful when the landlord turned them out.

'Ah, never mind!' said Erica. 'It's not too late for Crabb to turn up even now. He knows our house. He always was a bloody fly-by-night.'

'That's right,' said Johnny Hobbs. 'And think of this, gal – if he don't, there's always more fish in the sea, ain't there? And not all wrapped up in black rubber shrouds!'

It didn't help that Johnny Hobbs was joking, it didn't help at all. She already feared she might never see her man again.

Twenty

The entrance to Portsmouth Harbour is extremely narrow, with a fort on either shore. On the Hampshire side Fort Blockhouse, brick and square and brooding, and on Portsea Island the Round Tower of the ancient fortifications, stark white and strangely beautiful. It was on top of this that Commander Crabb stood, alongside Goddam Smith, to watch the might of Russia steaming in.

After they had docked, Smith told him, the plan would be to do a preliminary dive with an officer from *Vernon*, a Lieutenant Franklin, to 'work out the lie of the land.' Which sounded crazy.

'The lie of what land?' he wondered out aloud. 'Size of those fucking props, the water'll be solid mud for hours, won't it? Pea fucking soup. And what if they put guards out? Frogmen? That's what we do when we hit a foreign harbour, isn't it? As a warning, if nothing else.'

Goddam seemed to agree.

'A declaration of intent,' he said. 'A little itty-bitty warning. I tell you what, I'll call the prelim off, at least till later. Till things have settled down.'

Apart from anything else, though, Crabb didn't feel up to diving yet. It wasn't his hangover, he told himself – he had worse than that six times a week. But last night in the Sally Port he'd had his dream, the worst of any in his repertoire. He'd been below with Bill Bailey in the Med. They'd come across two Italians on a pig and they'd drawn their knives. Kill or be killed. It was a dream that haunted him. A fucking nightmare.

But the Navy salutes were starting now. No guns yet – the displays of mutual respect would kick off in London later when the top men met in their dickie bows to tell lies across the porcelain and crystal – but bosun's calls and bugles, and dipping flags and so on. There were crowds along the waterfront and there was cheering, though not much. Russia had helped us win the war, maybe, but now seemed keen enough to have another one. Willy-waggling, Crabb thought it. Who's got the biggest fucking nuke.

For all his headache and his rumbling gut, though, Crabbie was quite impressed with the way the warships looked. Decked over all with bunting, with a mass of saluting sailors and the band attempting an English march by way of friendship, they came in line ahead through the entrance under their own steam. The Admiralty tugs were there, but in the background, ready to bustle in at a second's notice if anything went wrong.

Smith, beside him, laughed quietly.

'That'd be a turn-up for the books, eh bub? That'd be a loss of face if they had to pull the biggest bastard off the shingle. How much spare water is there underneath her keel?'

Crabb could not remember, although he'd done his homework. John Henry, before he'd lost the leader job, had done it with him and kept him up to snuff. He barely remembered their names, now. Cruiser *Ordzhonikidze*, destroyers *Sovershenny* and *Smotryaschy*. Pronounciation? Hah!

Smith was smirking. He knew the answer, and he was going to rub it in.

'She draws about twenty three feet, loaded,' he said. 'If I remember rightly. Well, twenty two foot eight, let's say. Sixteen thousand, six hundred forty tons, at six hundred eighty nine feet by seventy two foot two. She's got a hundred eighteen thousand horsepower that gives her thirty two and a half knots – in your English money, that's thirty seven miles an hour. And four tenths.'

'How long's the stoker's cock?' said Buster, sourly. He felt ill. He could almost see the Sally Port Hotel from his position on the tower. He could almost smell the bar. 'Or didn't you get to hear the most important bits?'

'Yeah, smart,' said Smith happily. 'They'll be lying alongside South Railway jetty, side-by-side I guess.

Do you think that'll make your job easier or harder?'

Crabb picked up on this.

'Our job, you mean,' he said. 'Or are you—'

As if on cue, the Russian cruiser tore off a prolonged and mighty whistle blast. One long hoot to indicate that she was about to turn to starboard. But as the destroyers joined in immediately, it was in fact a form of riotous salute. Crabb was deafened. He could not even hear his own voice. Smith was grinning at him, toothily.

All Crabb knew, all that came back to him, was that this whole exercise was pointless. As John Henry had told him ruefully, the *Ordzhonikidze* was obsolete, rendered useless in modern naval warfare by the missiles and the jets that saw such dinosaurs as nothing but enormous targets, far too slow to get away.

He was going to dive down beneath her – on his own, it seemed – just to feed the egos of some secret service wallahs with a schoolboy sense of humour, or reality. He wondered why the Government thought it was a good thing. The PM needed kicking from arsehole to breakfast time for not banning it. Another public schoolboy, see? Another chinless Eton wonder. Eden had gone to Eton, hadn't he? Of course he had, they all had. Crabb fucking hated them.

And he was sure now he'd be going on his own. Oh, Sydney, he thought, you tried to bloody warn me. Oh, Syd.

Twenty One

Later that day there was to be a prelim dive after all, Crabb learned – voluntary but damn-all chance that he'd get out of it, although Smith had failed earlier to make him accept an invitation to join a party going on board the Russian ships for a 'little visit'.

'It's a courtesy!' the CIA man had told him. 'It's politeness, Buster, they want to let you see their ships! Ain't you Limeys meant to be polite? You can *not* say no!'

'Try me,' said Crabb.

'Okay, I will! Are you off your trike or something? You can mingle with 'em. Rub shoulders with the bastards. Smile at them and neck their vodka. And thinking all the time you're going to screw them over. You're going to rob their darkest secrets. The invite's from the captain. Maybe from Khrushchev him-fucking-self!'

Crabb was not impressed. Early next morning the waters of the harbour would be as black as pitch, and he had a cold feeling about it, deep underneath his hangover. The chances were that he would find damn all. Zero. Zilch.

The chances also were, that if he went on board the ships he might get recognized. He'd got the George Medal, for God's sake, and his picture had been in the papers quite often, and the Russians had the KGB. Wouldn't that be wonderful – to swan up to a gaggle of Red matelots and have them call him Buster? It might be ridiculous, but it made his blood run cold.

'Don't you get it yet Goddam? I'm not coming on no visit. If Khrushchev misses me, I'll send a little card.'

Smith had accepted with bad grace, but later, it appeared, he had colluded with Lieutenant Franklin, and a boat had been selected to ferry Crabb out to the waters near the Russians. Before he found this out, though, he'd returned to the hotel, taken a briefing phone call from the top dogs at HMS *Dolphin* across the water, and hit the pit. He rang Pat up first, but said that he was busy. He said he might get away that evening, but not to count on it. He said by tomorrow afternoon he'd be free as a bird.

'What about a sexy foursome?' he said. 'Is Erica up for it, d'you reckon? Hey Pat, that was a joke! That was a fucking joke! Listen, love, I'll see you tonight. I will, I fucking will!'

But she'd hung up, and come to think of it, he almost didn't care. He looked out of the window at the High Street, he looked down left to the Sally Port itself, he nodded his recognition at the bust of King Charles in his alcove on the wall. He could even remember the carved inscription under it.

'Having paffed through many dangers...' No, bugger it, the rest was gone. He'd only ever seen it full of booze. He'd *paffed* through many dangers himself, he thought, miserably. And in the morning he would *paff* through many more...

When he woke up he felt a little better, but not much. He freshened up and went down to reception, where he sat and tried to read a paper. Then he asked the woman where to take a walk – as if he didn't know this part of Pompey like the back of his hand – and she suggested the cathedral. It was only across the road but it was a bloody ugly pile and he'd never fancied it. During the war they'd built a wall across the back-end until the bombs died down a bit, and they'd never had the cash to finish it, apparently. Somehow, that seemed to him to sum Portsmouth up. A dump that wouldn't give a penny to a blind man.

But he wandered round a bit, re-read the inscription on King Charles, went through the Sally Port and wandered along the hot walls – wondering not for the first time what made them 'hot' – then walked down Broad Street and took the ancient chain ferry across to Gosport so that he could get a good view of the Russian ships from across the harbour. They looked very fine moored up along South

Railway. That night, he guessed, Khrushchev and his mate would hop a train and go and dine with Eden. The train would come right onto the jetty so they could step aboard like royalty. The fucking Reds were as bad as any other fuckers when it came to it.

By the time Crabb returned to the hotel he was bored titless, and ready for a drink. But Goddam was waiting for him with a fresh-faced young man in uniform, and Goddamn had a proposition.

'This is Lieutenant George Franklin, Buster—'

'But call me Frankie, sir. I—'

'He's a *Vernon* diving wallah and he's going to be your tender in the morning. And he's going to take us out now in a launch he's commandeered and you're going to have a peep at shapely bottoms. You want a scotch to set you up? Of course you do!'

'Anything,' laughed Crabb. 'Just get me in the water before I die of frigging boredom. Hi Frankie. Good to meet yer. Don't bloody call me sir.'

Franklin was an expert and efficient dresser, it turned out, and as Crabb slipped into the water late that afternoon, all three men felt full of confidence. They were only eighty yards or so from the stern of the *Ordzhonikidze,* and the tide was slack enough to cause no problems.

'Just look about a bit,' said Goddam. 'Make sure we've got your weighting right, and the new suit's comfortable. Try out the temperature and the light down there. Tomorrow you can take a lamp if need be.'

'And see if there's any Russians lurking,' Frankie Franklin joked. 'You never know with foreigners, do you? Make sure you've got your knife ready!'

Maybe it was the Grant's, maybe it was the dreams the night before, maybe it was the mention of enemies, but for Crabb the outing was disastrous. The measured breathing, the co-ordination of fins and muscles, the thousand other things he'd done unconsciously a thousand times – they all felt wholly wrong. The nearer he got to the three warships, the more horrible he felt. His even breaths began to jerk, his arms to tense, his clear, calm thoughts to go quite haywire.

'Oh God,' he told himself. 'Oh Syd. Oh Bill. Those poor Italians. Oh Bill, we killed them.'

Suddenly, completely, he was hallucinating. Was he off Gibraltar or was it Leghorn? Was this Bill Bailey, the man who'd chosen him, his mate and mentor, who went on to get the VC? They were in the Med for certain, and it was warm and pale, enough light down below to see the pig – the *maiale*, the chariot, the two-man submarine. Two-man pig, two pigs on top of it.

Not pigs, but frogmen. Italians. The men who'd started it, invented it, the bravest human beings that he had ever known.

It was the seventh of December in 1942. They had been dropping depth charges as usual, to flush out the pigs they thought were under there. Then they'd gone down, he and Bill or Syd or someone else, and seen the men. They'd been detached from the *maiale* but were still alive. Were they groggy? Were they stunned? He could not tell, he must not care. There as a war on.

And so they'd killed them. Cut their breathing pipes. Maybe stabbed one, he honestly could no longer say. And when their bodies had been found, he and Syd Knowles had won their swim fins. And dropped a wreath on to the water by way of thank you, and to mark their grave...

Although the tide was slack, Buster Crabb got into trouble. His weights were wrong, his buoyancy too negative, he was seeing visions. Below him was the mud of Pompey Harbour, the filthy, gloopy mud. All round him as the tide slid gently out were turds from Russkie arseholes, made up of spuds and sausages washed down with vodka and sweet tea. Ghosts, as well. Human forms in the dirty water, undulating.

Or maybe they were frogmen.

A moment later, Crabb banged into something, and missed a breath, and almost took in water round his mask and mouthpiece, and almost panicked. He did not, though, it was only almost. He'd been doing this for damn near twenty years, since bloody 'forty-one. Sixteen, at least. And he'd do sixteen more.

Or die in the attempt.

The divers' joke brought him back again, and he realised what had happened. The tide had pushed him up against a pile, vertical, weed-covered, barnacle-encrusted, slimy. The piling for the railway station pier, for certain. Kick away upstream, turn left, push off and upwards, smartish. Above him, not so far away, would be his launch with good old Good Goddam and Georgie Frankie Franklin. Jesus, they owed him a bloody drink. Did they bloody ever!

But when he broke surface, and they grabbed his arms, and pulled him alongside and half into the boat and helped him tear his mask off, all he said was, 'Not so bad, lads. Need a bit less weight around me waist. And a half a pint of fucking whisky.'

But his face, however, was as white as bone. Both Smith and Franklin noticed it. And neither said a word.

Twenty Two

Commander Lionel Crabb, perhaps, had been far more shaken by that afternoon than he was able to admit. When they reached the Sally Port Hotel again, both Goddam Smith and Frankie Franklin were more than ready to go on the booze, and he was not.

They fell upon the bar like two marauding Huns.

'A big one for the hero!' shouted Smith. 'A giant! Never mind a double, take a pint glass and see what it'll hold! Franklin, what's yours? It's on James Jesus Angleton!'

There was no one else in the bar yet, but walls have ears, the posters said. Crabb felt irrationally angry. Irrationally? It wasn't these mouthy bastards that were going to fucking die, was it?

'Get me a taxi,' he said. But the manager had entered, with a surprise.

'You don't need one, Mr Crabb,' he said. 'Ted's ordered it; Mr Davis. A car from *Vernon* to take you anywhere you like. Free. On the Royal Navy. A courtesy.'

'Yoo-hoo!' yelled Frankie. 'That's the way to do it, Crabb! Where are we going? Where d'you want to drink?'

Crabb turned on him, snarling.

'I'm going where I'm going, and you can fuck yourself. And you, Smith. I'm going out to get a bit of company. Call me a taxi!'

And then he stopped.

'No, belay that, I'll bloody walk. I'm not a Yankee, am I? I'm going to bloody walk.'

Franklin moved as if to stop him, but a look from Goddam cut that off. Crabb went from the lobby into the High Street like a streak of furious lightning. Twelve minutes later he was at the Harbour Station.

'Where's he gone?' asked the lieutenant. 'Should I go after him?'

'I know where he's gone,' said Goddam Smith. 'That's why I get more pay than you.'

'Oh. We've got diving in the morning, sir.'

'He'll be back,' said Smith. 'I'll send a car for him. Just make sure you get his weights right this time.'

* * *

On the Soviet ship, there was not an argument. There may have been opinions, but there was not an argument. The discussion took place in an armoured alcove off the inner bridge, and it lasted for some time, while Moscow was consulted. The commissar was the mouthpiece, and it was his decision not to tell Comrade Khrushchev or the Comrade Prime

Minister of what had been decided.

It was his decision, also, that they were not informed of the suspicions raised by the officer of the watch that the British were engaged in underwater spying.

'They should be told,' the captain said. 'Surely, *tovarich*, they have the right to—'

He was powerful, the captain, but not as powerful as the Party man. The decision was political. Only one man could take it. Only one man had that level of responsibility. The captain shut his mouth.

'What was seen? A motor boat,' said the commissar. 'Any divers? Possibly. How far away? Up to a hundred metres. And then the vessel slunk away. And you think that that might make Comrade Khrushchev shake with fear?'

Two juniors dared to smile. One even made a small noise of amusement.

'But you are right,' the commissar continued. 'It is not a minor matter. I need a briefing on your level of surveillance. Watchfulness. How many men you can deploy under water, their levels of training and of competence. How many sharpshooters you are planning to position. On which decks and where.'

The captain and his senior officers had been over this many times as the *Ordzhonikidze* had ploughed down from the north. They were competent and confident. The only matter was...

'We need most guidance, Comrade Commissar,' said the captain, 'on the level of force we must apply should it be necessary. If one of our frogmen, for example, met one of theirs – should the enemy be killed?'

'The enemy? Britain was our honoured partner in the war. We are friends, not enemies.'

Frosty smiles. The juniors this time dared to almost chuckle.

'But you are right once more, Comrade Captain.' It was the commissar's refrain; he must not make decisions that were officially in the officer's domain. 'You are right to seek guidance, and I in turn have taken it. And there are several options, it would seem. To kill, to capture. To capture then to kill, and dispose of later in the far Atlantic. To capture, question, even to try to turn.'

'To turn, comrade?'

'To make their frogmen see the error of their ways. To educate them in their misguided views. Of their own society, and of our way. The Union of Soviet Socialist Republics. One hero turned, of whatever nation, is the ultimate triumph. Is that not so?'

And truth to tell, the captain thought but did not say, we know their frogmen have an expertise that we would give our eye-teeth for. A triumph and a prize of greatest price.

He turned to his chief adjutant, indicating a sheaf of papers they had worked on in the last twelve hours. A detailed plan for observing and for searching.

'I would be honoured, *tovarich*, if you would consider this,' he said. 'I understand, of course, that the greatest goal is peace, and we are not here to "rock the boat," as men of the English Navy say. But if it must be rocked...'

He passed the sheaf across the table. The commissar regarded it. And indicated to his own adjutant.

'Good,' he said. 'I think we are agreed. If all else fails, no body must be found.'

* * *

Pat Rose had been so sure he would not turn up, that she burst into tears when Lionel Crabb walked into the snug bar of the Robin Hood. He looked so calm and normal in his tweeds, so sober, so pleased to see her. And she'd been drinking gin, which often made her cry. Mother's ruin, they called it up in Streatham. But she'd never been a mother, poor old Pat. Too late now.

'Christ,' said Johnny Hobbs, 'look what the cat's brought in! You know how to make a lady smile, mate! What you having?'

'Your suit!' said Erica. 'Eh, aren't you dapper,

Crabbie! Can I try your hat on?'

'Lionel!' wailed Pat. 'Oh Lionel, love, you'll be the death of me. Where you been?'

'I said he'd turn up, didn't I?' said Erica. 'Oh gawd, that was last night, though! Oh well, better late than never, eh? How did you get here? Did you come by train?'

He had, but by now he was too far down his first pint of bitter to bother to reply. It was Gales, from the brewery just down the road in Horndean, a smashing country pint, not like London rubbish. He drank so fast it hardly touched the sides.

'Why you crying, love?' he said at last. 'I told you it'd be all right, didn't I? I told you not to be a silly girl.'

It was not as riotous as the night before had been – there wasn't any singing for a start – but they had a damned good time. The only bad bit was when Pat, in a rush of tipsy love, began to talk about the great big bed that Erica had made up for them. She knew him well. His face changed. She knew him too well.

'You've got to go, haven't you? You've got to go off back to Sally Port.'

'Sally who?' said Erica. 'You lousy bastard, Crabb! You lousy, rotten pig!'

But Pat was off the gin now, and the weeps had been extinguished. She was tough enough to make a better joke than that.

'Balls to Sally, he'd rather kip with Smudger Smith,' she told her friend. 'You always said he was a poofter, didn't you? He's going for a wankie with a Yankie!' They laughed so hard they almost died, or cried. And when Lieutenant Frankie Franklin turned up in a naval car to take him back to Pompey, they bought a round for the whole bar.

'Did you tell him you were here?' said Erica. 'Now that's a wasted opportunity, you silly bugger, Pat said we'd have a funny foursome!'

'I didn't tell him,' Crabbie said. 'He's a medium – he sees into the future. He's medium drunk to three quarters arseholed, and he's driving me back down to Point to do me bleeding duty. Bottoms up!'

'Oh, love,' said Pat Rose, finally. 'I wish you wasn't going, Lionel. You will be back tomorrow, won't you? Promise me.'

'I will,' said Lionel. He felt sentimental. He felt full of love. He felt invincible. He kissed her wetly on the mouth and raised a cheer all round the bar. 'I promise you.'

It was closing time when they got back to the Sally Port Hotel, but they were *bona fides* so it didn't matter. Goddam was in the bar but only sipping, and Crabb was having none of that. When Franklin pointed out they were due to be picked up to dive at five o'clock next morning, he shifted up a gear. He changed his order from a single to a double Scotch, with a pint of Brickwoods for a chaser.

Smith and Frankie drank very slowly, Crabb very fast. One pint and one double down, he set them up again immediately, and when Smith demurred, he drank his Scotch himself. And then his own. After four doubles more, Goddam told him to ease off, and got a mouthful of abuse so vile that Crabb was banned from having one more drop. He stormed off to his bedroom, where he said he had a 'fucking bottle'.

And at five a.m., to everyone's astonishment, he was first into the dining room to have a cup of coffee. Unfortunately for the gesture of bravado, he could hardly lift it to his lips for shaking. He was led into the car by two strong naval ratings, and one of them had to light his first fag of the day for him.

Twenty Three

It was much too early for Nick Elliott to learn of things like this, because there were strict rules and protocol. Marion Wilson was the first to get the nod that something was happening, through channels that she still found quite unsettling. The green telephone on her desk buzzed once, and an unknown man said 'Claret has been poured'.

Marion, who felt that she had aged quite rapidly in the past few days, thought Claret was a silly codename anyway, and had to bite back a comment that would have been considered pert.

'Wilco,' she forced herself to say, and even that sounded ridiculous. She picked up her private line to Elliott's home, then put it down again. It was not even eight o'clock. He would positively roast her.

In an adjoining office, she found some operatives she knew were in on the operation, and sounded them out to see if they had heard. No. But they agreed her boss might still be fast asleep. He liked his bed, did Nicholas.

Then she tried the switchboard. Marion had learned a lot in recent days, some of which her superiors would have been surprised to know themselves. Sometimes the humblest had the best intelligence, which they would disseminate only to the equally humble. She knew the duty switchboard girl, it turned out; they had had tea and cakes together in a Lyons Corner House only the week before. The call, she learned, had come from Portsmouth. Three men in a dinghy had gone 'below,' or were about to.

'Three Men in a Boat, that's funny isn't it?' she said. 'Like in the film.'

'The film?' said Marion. 'I've read the book, but there's not a film, is there? Who's in it?'

'Jimmy Edwards, Laurence Harvey, David—'

'Laurence Harvey? Oooh, I like him! Where's it on?'

'Well it's not out yet, is it? It's due for Christmas. It's got that Shirley Eaton in it, too. My boyfriend... Well, less said about that the better, eh!'

They could have nattered on, but the switchboard was livening up for the morning, and Marion had made a decision. If the men were in the harbour, or getting close to it,

Elliott would have to know, whatever. If 'C' should hear from anybody else, or – oh my gosh, what if Mr Eden...?

Twenty five minutes later Nick Elliott was in his limousine and on his way. Less than half an hour from call to off. That's how urgent it was. Extraordinary.

As the waters closed over Crabbie, he felt an almost holy sense of peace. In fact, he contemplated slipping his finger into the corner of his diving mask and just breathing in. People said that drowning was an easy way to die, though God knows how they thought they knew. But it was peaceful down here, no doubt of that. The sea was dark and strangely warm, and sleep a lovely possibility.

He had been quite right about his 'dive-buddy,' as Goddam Smith had called himself. He was not a buddy, and had no intention of going on the dive, although the sea inside the harbour was much calmer than the day before. In the boathouse by King's Stairs he had climbed into his silks and woollen long johns, presumably just for show – and had the cheek to laugh because Buster had his on already, had probably even 'slept in the goddam things.'

But after that, the Yank dropped all pretence. His fins, his oxygen cylinder, his rebreathing bag lay in a heap, and one of the naval ratings took charge of them. Unlike Smith, Crabb let no one touch his gear at all.

'Fuck off,' he growled at one sailor. 'You're messing with my fucking life.' He was a professional. That's how he stayed alive.

For reasons of presumed secrecy, they clambered into a twelve-foot Navy dinghy instead of any sort of motor boat. It was small and quiet, certainly, with an unnamed lieutenant commander at the oars, plus the frogmen and Frankie Franklin. No one was talking, until about two hundred feet offshore Crabb asked for a cigarette. The officer forbade it, in a snappish whisper, and Smith said in an anguished voice, 'Crabbie, they'll see the light!'

'No smoke, no dive,' said Buster Crabb. 'It's up to you, boys. Without a snout Crabbie ain't going nowhere.'

'Sir to you,' the officer snapped, and Franklin gave a nervous laugh. 'Oh fuck,' said Crabbie. 'What a gang of toe-rags.'

The lighter flared, however – shielded like a holy relic – and he dragged deeply on the Navy Cut.

'Great little coffin nail,' he coughed. 'The tobacco that counts.'

By the time the fag was done, the dinghy was as near the cruiser as they dared to go. The sky was black and misty and they could make out no watchers on the decks above them, but their nerves were stretched to breaking point. Not Crabb's though. He twitched out his dog-end, flicked it overboard, secured his nose-clip, took his mouthpiece between his lips and clamped his face mask on.

They watched him twist the valve on the cylinder strapped across his stomach, adjust his counter-lung, and do his final checks. Inside his mask, smoke was still visible, with him smiling through the murk. Smiling or coughing. He is insane, thought Goddam Smith. He is utterly insane.

Crabb clambered like an animal into the stern, then suddenly became elegant. Almost in an instant he had half rolled sideways in a fluid movement, swung his legs over the gunwale, spun half-round to face the transom, then slipped into the water up to his neck. A few more adjustments, a quick thumbs-up – and he was gone. A half a second later a flipper kicked through the surface for an instant. Beyond that there was nothing.

Buster Crabb was breathing oxygen so he left no bubbles. Buster Crabb had disappeared.

* * *

Time in London, for Marion, was standing still. Half an hour after Elliott had left his house, she heard the first hints that something, possibly, might just be going wrong. And she heard it, shamefully, from a contact in the opposition – a typist in MI5.

'What do you mean, Charlotte?' she said. 'Who told you this? I've never even heard of Buster Crabb.'

'Ha ha ha,' her friend replied. 'Come on Marion, it's only me. We got it off that American who went down with him. He's one of ours.'

'American? Yours? What, not Bernard Smith, surely?'

'Bernard, Matthew, Goddam – you call him what you like, love. He's one of Angleton's. He's in the goddamn CIA!'

'Oh Christ,' said Marion. 'Oh shit, oh heavens! Who knows this? In your lot? You haven't told them, have you?'

But Charlotte could not lie. Matthew Smith – or a messenger from him – had been in touch indeed, not long ago. He'd gone right to the top, to Dick White. Sir Dick had been horrified. Or, she suspected secretly, overjoyed.

'It's all right, dear,' she mocked her friend. 'Officially we heard it from MI6. Hasn't Tricky Nicky come in yet? It's nearly—'

Marion looked at the wall clock. Time was going mad.

'But what does Sir Dick—? He and Nick Elliott don't even—'

'It's a wonderful chip for bargaining though, isn't it? Mr Smarmy Elliott's head on a plate. And his lights and liver.'

'It can't true,' said Marion. 'It's a silly, silly...it's a rumour on the grapevine, your people live and die by gossip. I promise you, Charlotte, it isn't true.'

She slammed the phone down. And when Elliott faced her ten minutes later, he confirmed that she'd been right.

'Bit of a silly blip,' he told her, blandly. 'One

rumour, and the system crashes in flames as usual. Dick White thinks he knows something that I don't, the damned buffoon. I can promise you, my poppet, it won't stand up on its hind feet.'

'Yes sir,' said Marion, her breast still heaving. 'I realized it must have been. A silly blip. They are such *rumour* mongers!'

'Headless chickens. Good God, the man isn't due in the water for an hour yet, and he's got air for absolutely ages. Buster Crabb is fine and dandy, you mark my words. He's indestructible!'

Twenty Four

The first time Crabb was seen from the Russian ships, it was by a young sharpshooter stationed on a destroyer. But the orders had been disseminated from the *Ordzhonikidze,* and the sailor knew enough about hierarchy not to be the man to break a protocol. The ratings on the cruiser considered it to be their show, and for him to fire the first shot would be the act of an idiot.

As was the Soviet way, the orders themselves were also horribly ambiguous. Shoot to kill if necessary, the marksmen had been told, the level of necessity being the privilege of each sniper to decide. Life and death then, possibly. For the shooter and the shot.

It was, though – and this was very lucky, he considered – not a clear shot to pull off. The black surface of the harbour was rippled, the ebb tide had started running, and the light spilling from the cruiser moored alongside dappled the water between the ships so that the picture seemed to move.

What he had thought might be a swim fin breaking through might just as well have been a trick of light; or indeed a fish. As soon as they had moored the afternoon before, the sailors had noticed them, great big fat lazy things hanging round for scraps. Filth-eaters, they called them back at home.

'Piotr!' he hissed, to his companion. 'Piotr, did you see that thing?'

'What thing? Where? I saw nothing.'

Good. He breathed out gently.

'Nothing,' he said. 'Me too. Back to sleep, Piotr!'

'Evgeny – go fuck yourself.'

The Russian 'combat divers' – four of them – were on the *Ordzhonikidze* and would go out in relays, it had been decided. That way the surveillance could be constant, without fear of a hiatus in case of depleted oxygen. The cruiser did not have a diving hatch cut in the hull, nor were the frogmen considered fully competent. In some ways they were only playing catch-up in this game.

Their lead was Eduard Koltsov, picked as much for his bravery as his skill. At 23 he was an arrogant young man, proud of the long, curved dagger he wore by special dispensation. The other three were worse than useless, in his view. If there were British divers out today, it was he alone who'd deal with them.

Despite the calmness of the sea, he was nervous. The briefings the night before had emphasized the speed at which the ebb could run – up to four knots on a spring tide – and if anything went wrong one could be whisked out through the harbour entrance like shit out of a goose, as his *babushka* would have put it. Down the harbour, through the entrance, into the Solent and Spithead.

He laughed to himself. I might end up on the Isle of Wight, he thought. I wonder if they'd let me be an honourable defector! I wonder what the beer's like.

He checked his watch, for the umpteenth time. If no word came from the observers up aloft, he'd have to go soon. To check it out. To feel the waters. To tell the others what they might expect.

The idiots.

Many feet beneath him, by coincidence, Crabbie was thinking of the Italian mother-ship of 'forty-two, the *Olterra*. An oil tanker interned for the duration, she was the base at Algeciras from which the frogmen of the Tenth Flotilla – *Decima MAS* – ran the pigs to put the limpet mines on the British ships off Gib.

On HMS *Cormorant*, the Navy's shore base under the Rock, he'd used to sit with Bill Bailey, Dave Bell and the others, and fantasise about the cushy equipment and facilities the Italians enjoyed. Pop out of the secret air-lock, hop on a two-man torpedo, and chug across to Gib with the detachable warhead and a limpet or two for luck. While him and his muckers had to go out in overalls and plimsolls, and breath through Davis escape equipment from the ark. The Italians got vino, too. Gallons of it.

Close enough to see the Russkie hulls half clearly,

Crabb switched his mind from neutral and began to plan. His job was to check the props and rudders of the *Ordzidooflop*, just in case. In case of what, he had no real idea, but then again neither did the spooks who'd put him on the job, for a certainty. His head was crashing with the booze – made much worse by the pressure and the suck and blow – and he wouldn't have said no to a quick chuck-up and a crap. Diving was a mug's game. Diving in the condition he was in was bloody stupid. Daft.

The hull was long and curved and bulbous. He tried to remember some of the capacities that Goddam had told him of inside her guts. Enough shells and high explosive to blow Pompey off the map, maybe. Or maybe bloody not. Enough weed and slime and shit to choke a hungry whale. He wondered if they ever took her into dock to scrub her down. Why bother, though? She was waiting for the scrapheap. She wasn't worth a wank.

The knife between his legs was getting in the way, a bit. It was a very long knife he carried, almost as good as his crabhead swordstick, but ten times better for stabbing Russians with – or cutting through old cables and prising limpet mines off steel. It was long, and dangled from his waist and swung around sometimes, and buggered up his swimming action. He missed his swordstick. He'd shown it off last night in the Robin Hood. They'd been dead impressed.

There was something else unwieldy on this dive, but he couldn't for the moment remember what. That was worrying. Why not remember? Too early for the gas to get at him. Too shallow for God's good oxygen to start playing silly buggers. And then it came to him. A camera. Oh yeah, with a lamp, an' all. He shook his head, and looked around for it.

It was on his wrist. Yes, there it was. Another bloody dangler to slow him down. Someone had stuck it in his hand before he'd left the dinghy, that officer who'd done the rowing and had a plum right up his bum, or talked like it. The latest thing, apparently, cooked up by the Navy science boys. So he was due to photograph, was he? Some bloody hopes they had of that! He couldn't even use a box Brownie properly, Pat said.

Pat. Ah, Pat. He'd tried to get a shot of her on the bed one time, he'd tried to get her in her undies to do a sexy pose. She'd told him to sod off. What was it with women? What did they want out of life? Both Pat and his first wife had just been barmaids once, but you'd have thought that they were Lady Muck. Ideas above their station, both of them. What was wrong with a good old bit of filth? He'd never understand them, women.

He was underneath her belly now, the Russian cruiser's, in fronds and waves of seaweed, brown and green and slimy. But her keel was there, easy to follow from one end to the other. He wondered how deep the keel went. Goddam Smith had told him but that was gone as well. He hoped it wasn't thirty feet or more. OP. Oxygen Pete. The silent bloody killer. He counted backwards, ten to zero. That felt all right. He thought. Maybe he'd try again. Yes, that would be a good idea. What would?

Up on the surface, Goddam and the officer sat in awkward silence. It's a British thing, thought Goddam Smith. This asshole officer won't even give his name, and

Frankie Franklin can't talk to him because his rank's too low. How did the bastards ever win the war? Maybe the Krauts were worse.

The morning was getting beautiful. Despite the bomb-sites – and there were more of them than a Yankee believed possible ten years beyond the war – it was still an interesting town. Well, the harbour was. Stretching north and narrow, lined on either side with mothballed warships tethered to gigantic buoys, even the frigging *Victory* sitting upright in her dry dock in the middle of the Dockyard, you'd think the Germans could have bombed it, wouldn't you? Christ knows, they must have tried!

And the Gosport side, the bit that Buster called Turktown but couldn't tell him why. With the pale diving escape tower sticking in the sky and the submarines on trots all down the *Dolphin*, near Fort Blockhouse.

He wondered what the Russians made of it. He wondered if they were in the harbour now, creeping round the *Ordzhonikidze* and the *Sovershenny* and *Smotryaschy* looking for poor old Crabbie. He wondered how that funny little *hombre* with his funny clothes and hat would say their names.

Smith looked at his watch. He'd been underwater for fifteen minutes now, had Crabb, and even in the comfort of the dinghy it felt like fifteen hours.

Don't time fly when you're happy, Goddam thought. Don't time fly.

Twenty Five

In the offices, Marion was in a state of suspended animation. Time for her, rather than flying, was standing absolutely still. All round her men were behaving normally – smoking, drinking coffee, one vile Navy Int man necking breakfast Scotch.

Not behaving normally, though, in reality. Contingency planning. Lying to themselves, and everybody else.

What if it's gone wrong? What if it's gone tits up? Who can we blame? Who's going to be the fall-guy to tell Eden? Sir John Sinclair, the boss man of SIS, was out of the country, which to Marion somehow seemed inevitable. How did they do it, she wondered? But they always did.

And the Russians will be dining up in Town tonight, all stuffed-shirts together, all itching to start another war. She wondered somehow how the 'new peace' could survive. How long.

In other parts of the building, other men were planning their salvations or assessing if there were advancement possibilities. Ian Fleming, on a 'casual' visit as so often, was talking about Khrushchev and fine silk underwear, Kim Philby, in the name of 'Peach', was contacting Moscow for the latest update. Elliott was wondering what would be the proper line to take if something did go wrong, and who would be the best man for dreaming up a cover.

'Nothing to do with us,' that was the normal formula. 'Regrettable but there's been a lack of proper supervision. In any case, it's all completely innocent, whatever's happened. Or thought to have happened, rather. We're in the process of investigating. With the utmost rigour. And if need be – this can be said without fear or favour! – heads will roll. And lessons will be learned.'

Down in Portsmouth, a dreamlike state was creeping in. On the surface, in the shadows, a twelve-foot dinghy with three men sitting silently, as lovely sunlight spread across the dark green waters of the harbour. Gosport ferries steaming from side to side, jammed with workers. Naval pinnaces roaring between the 'stone frigates,' the *Vernon*, *Dolphin*, *Excellent*. And on the Russian ships, thousands of sailors having breakfast. While snipers studied waves and water.

Below the surface, Eduard Koltsov caught his first sight of the alien, and his heart leapt. So it was true! The English were below the ships, stealing secrets from the Motherland! Great joy – and then the enemy was gone again. Koltsov eased his long knife in its scabbard and kicked out towards the great ship's belly. The man would not escape.

Buster Crabb had not seen Koltsov and, frankly, he was indifferent. Time underwater can lose normal meaning, he well knew. The day before, on his practice dive, when he'd found himself jammed up against the piling of the railway jetty, he felt that he'd been below for hours, ages, half a bloody week. In fact he'd used up twenty minutes' worth of oxygen and had an hour left. It was a mystery.

Breathing oxygen under water had other little mysteries, too. It left no tell-tale bubbles on the surface, which was the good part, and the water today felt warm enough for anything. Was that relevant?

How long had he been down, then, since he'd slipped off the transom of the dinghy? Five minutes? Two? Twenty? Ages? He had a watch on, naturally, with a great big fucking screen on it, like Big Ben or the Pompey Guildhall clock. He felt a giggle rise. The Krauts had bombed that to buggery, and he could no more see his watch than he could fly. Hey, Lionel, he thought, this feels so good.

An alarm bell rang inside his brain. Lionel? But his name was Crabbie, maybe Buster, Lionel Kenneth, sometimes Ken, that was what his wife had called him, his wife, but almost no one else. Who'd called him Lionel, then, just then inside his head? Oh shit, *he* had. Oh shit. This was much too early.

Hallucinations had always been a part of it for Crabbie. Oxygen was good, we all know that, but do not breathe it under pressure. He'd given lectures, for God's sake, he was the expert. He'd told dozens of rookies about it at the bloody diving tower. His mind went off again. With her head tucked underneath her arm – she walks the bloody tower. 'Enery the Eighth I am I am. Oh shit. How far down am I?

Now the water did feel cold, and he was freezing. Pompey Harbour was a bastard like that, even in high summer. When the sun shone on the mudflats up at Portchester and Flathouse, and up Fareham Creek, the sea warmed up like mother's milk, but the currents made the deep bits spit out streams of icy cold that could clench your lungs up, even through Pirelli's best. And he was near the entrance. He was alongside South Railway Jetty, in the deepest bit, where battleships and cruisers could moor up. The *ArchybollockyRusskifusskeree*, to name but one. Yeah, that was it, he was here to check her bottom out. Her dirty bits.

All humour died. Like he would, if he wasn't careful. Pull yourself together, Crabb, he thought. You're not down far enough to get OP. He told the rookies all about it every time.

'You'll call him Pete,' he'd say, 'and you'll think he is your friend. He ain't. He's going to kill you. He'll creep up on you and get you when you least expect it, it's a bit like whisky, only not so dear. Whisky is the devil, the man once said. OP is worse. However sweet the water, in the Med say, or off of Florida, he's waiting for you. You go down thirty feet you'll be all right. Maybe. You go down thirty two, you're fucked.'

He also told them that it sometimes hurt.

'Sometimes it's agony, the poison kills your guts. Sometimes it's almost friendly. Sometimes it gives you funny kind of dreams. Frogmen's corpses have been lifted off the bottom by their handles, if you get my meaning. The wife's best friend.'

The water had got bloody bitter. April was on the cusp of spring and winter, but no one had told Pompey it should be warming up. His hands and feet were bone-cold, he could feel his body turning into ice.

I welcome it, he thought. It's a lovely easy way to go. I've been there before, not once but many times. What about the Tobermory galleon? Jesus, but that was a cold one, no mistake. If you get cold enough, it feels like sleep. Now what am I down here for? Where am I?

A fish moved past his facemask; slowly, but it made him jump. It was a big fish, a horse mackerel they called them, he didn't have a notion why. Maybe it could eat a horse? No, that was wrong. They were so big, they said, because they lived on shit. A thousand ratings on a battleship or cruiser, and sometimes more. All shitting into Portsmouth Harbour for the lucky mackerel. Then matelots chucked a hook over and pulled them up and ate them in their turn. Charming, eh?

I'm down here, he told himself, to look at the rudders and propellors, and her keel and stuff. Any mods. Any new bits. Any mystery holes like on the *Sverdlov* that I done with Syd. My God, there was a real diving buddy! Oh bloody hell, why wouldn't he come with me this time? Oh Syd, oh Syd, of ye of little faith!

He knew damn well why Syd Knowles had ducked out, because it was no secret. Syd was thirty four and thought that that was getting on a bit for diving on the oxygen. And he was forty seven, and even the Navy had kicked him out. Until, of course, they needed a man to do a job like this. A job, as Elliott had told him, with a gallon of champagne to ease the pain, that was of *'incredible importance, Crabbie. Incalculable.'*

Hmm, thought Crabb. Champagne. Sham Pain. Nick Elliott was a liar and a fucking cheat. What was the point of swimming underneath a shagged-out old ship that would be in the scrapyard in a year or two? What had Goddam Smith said? Thirty knots? And how fast did jets go now? She'd not last ten minutes in a fight.

'You're being conned, mate,' he told himself. 'Syd's

right, you're past it, Crabbie. If you get out of this one, chum, you're giving up, okay? You'll marry Pat, you'll settle down, and Syd can be best man. You've fucking had it.'

A half a minute later, his brain still hazy, still seeing shadows and thinking half-formed thoughts, weird and fantastical, Crabb inadvertently broke the surface between two of the Russian ships. It was a shock when he realised what he'd done, because he felt that he was deeper. His head hurt. It hurt like hell. He hoped that Oxygen Pete was not crawling through his blood.

And on the foredeck of the *Sovershenny*, Piotr jumped almost out of his skin. 'Evgeny! There's someone in the water!'

'I told you! I told you! Piotr! We must shoot!'

'Stop!' It was a voice across the water, from the foredeck of the *Ordzhonikidze*. 'We have him. Leave it. He is ours.'

Evgeny could see a swirl of bubbles. Black rubber breaking through the surface.

Piotr was glaring murder.

And on the other ship, a man they knew called Ivan. His rifle was at his shoulder.

Ivan, the crack shot of the whole flotilla.

'Thanks, *tovarich*, I have him in my sights. So, better luck next time!' Piotr and Evgeny swore.

Twenty Six

Timing, when you're breathing oxygen, is a very fluid thing, as Goddam Smith well knew. He was by no means worried about Crabb, he told himself, but he was lying and he knew that, too. He'd been below for a long time, and it was almost time that he came up. Franklin was also getting restless. Only the lieutenant commander seemed indifferent. Why should he care?

If he doesn't come up again, thought Goddam, what then? How long do I wait before I press the panic button, and what else do I do? Row around in the dinghy as if I'm on a pleasure jaunt? Stick my head below the surface to see what I can see? Get my fins on and go overside? After about an hour, the Navy officer, unexpectedly, had suggested they might make a move, and Smith had overruled him.

'Too soon,' he said decisively. 'Don't think that you outrank me, bud, because you don't. We stay here till I say to go.'

The officer was not short of courage, or contempt.

'If we go ashore right now we might be able to help your man,' he said. 'At the very least we can shout up the alarm. If he stays down there much longer, he drowns.'

The CIA man did not argue.

'We stay,' he said. 'I'm the expert, and we stay. Even if he don't come up at all, it don't mean that he's dead. Only if we see a body is he dead. There's all sorts of things can go on down there that you don't know about. Got that?'

Like what, he wondered? Could they capture him? Could they get him on board the ships without us knowing? Of course they could. MI5 had said he might be a defector, among other things. Or he might have been kidnapped, for want of a better word. They could nab him, drug him, lock him up in chains and take him back to Russia. Black Lubyanka for a bit of crafty torture. He felt sorry for Buster Crabb. He felt really sorry.

But it was not time to worry, yet, not time at all. He looked at his watch and thought hard. Impossible to tell on oxygen. And no bodies had come bobbing to the surface. No body. Nobody. No-one.

He did not call the whole thing off until two hours had elapsed, or slightly more. It was full daylight now, and the Portsmouth Harbour ebb was running ever faster. All three on board the dinghy had been scanning the waves clandestinely, seeing – and saying – nothing.

I must tell London, Smith thought. I must tell Navy Intelligence, warn the local police not to raise a fuss. I must sort out the hotel register.

Back on shore, he stripped off his diving silk and pulled on trousers, shirt and jacket. A car whisked him to the Sally Port Hotel, where he called the manager into the back office and told him what he needed. The manager admired Americans – they didn't 'piss about' – and he was well aware there was some sort of operation going on. He collected the book, and watched in silence as Goddam tore out the page he'd signed the day before.

'We weren't here, check?' the CIA man said. 'Mister Smith and Mister Crabb, you've—'

'Never heard of, sir.' He dared a joke. 'I don't allow unknown men to sign as Mr Smith in any case. It can lead to all sorts of funny business!'

'You're good, goddamn it, sir – you're very good. And one more thing. The Press might somehow get a sniff of this. Might offer money. And you—'

'Know nothing, sir. Humphrey Bogart. Schtum!'

They ended on a laugh. Four hours later, when two MI5 men turned up from London to collect the same page, the manager had perfected the art of winking behind his hand, with a saucy roll of eye. Who knows, they might even have been impressed.

Beneath the cruiser, Eduard Koltsov took far too long to catch up with the frogman. And when he was close enough, he could hardly believe his eyes. Was it a child? Was it a circus midget? For an instant it made him feel quite bad. So small, so humble, so completely unaware.

But so British. Thus, according to the commissar, an evil man in fact, a murderer and educated at a school for spies called Eton. An awful school. The English are a very awful race.

So he moved in for the kill, his breathing regular and calm, his long knife very, very sharp. The man so small, his oxygen supply so vulnerable. He will sever them with one great sweep, the water will rush into the man's lungs.

It will be almost instantaneous. He does not want the man to see his death approaching. The man will hardly feel a thing.

The airline is beckoning. The blade begins its sweep.

* * *

The offices of MI5 and MI6 were hives of mania. They buzzed and throbbed with men wielding bits of paper to show they were engaged in business of unutterable importance. Peter Wright, a young spy fascinated by the innate lunacy of the game they played so seriously – and who later wrote a book about it which the Government spent millions trying to ban – moved from room to room, office to office, as a mesmerised observer.

He found Sir Dick White, a man of almost legendary charm, sitting in a daze, surrounded by others in a state of panic. He was asking for opinions from the highest to the lowest of them, and listening to none.

'Cummins,' he said several times. 'He'll have to give a hand to SIS. This may be all their fault, but as a mess it could rebound on all of us. It must be buried, kicked into the long grass. I'll have to go and talk to Eden. Lord alone knows what he's going to say. It was *verboten*!'

'We need to square it at that hotel in Portsmouth,' said another. 'We need to send men down to cover tracks.'

'But it's SIS, not us. Can't we just let them stew?'

'Smith's not SIS, he's CIA,' put in a third. 'And he works for us as well. He's MI5 if anything, not MI6.' He spread two hands out in a gesture. 'If anything,' he repeated. 'That's the key, sir. Anything.'

A fourth said: 'And anyway, Goddam did the Sally Port himself. He says we've got to nobble the Portsmouth police now, a Superintendent Lamport. And Admiral Inglis says we need to cross some palms with silver, reporters' palms, and he should know – he's boss of Naval Int. One of the big wheels on the local paper was in the RNVR, apparently, a fat man called Taff Symons, the editor maybe. He'll be on our side.'

'And what about the Reds?' asked Sir Dick. His mind, apparently, had begun to work again. 'What if they saw something? What if they had their own men in the water?'

There was a chilling pause. Things were sinking in.

'What if they captured him?' said Sir Dick. 'Or even killed him? Oh, sweet holy Jesus Christ.'

In Elliott's department – as befitted a cadre who had gone almost to a man to Cambridge via Eton – an aura of calm was quietly returning. They picked over possibilities, and polished up their stories as to what had really happened.

'What we must insist,' said Elliott, 'is that Crabb was engaged in testing some underwater apparatus which had nothing to do with the Russians, or indeed with any weaponry. Let's say sonar, shall we? For the improvement of Asdic on our latest submarines?'

'But why didn't we set up a rescue operation?' asked Marion. 'I mean, if it was legitimate and a man had disappeared we'd surely—?'

'We'll put it out there was one,' he replied. 'Good point, Miss Wilson. We'll acknowledge there was a Navy man involved and he messed it up. No one too high up, though, we can't let people think our top men are incompetent. Wasn't there a lieutenant commander on the diving team? He'll do. We'll let the Navy take the rap.'

'I'll have him sent back to his ship, sir,' said a young male aid. 'Not in disgrace exactly, but pending an enquiry. That should do the trick. Serious error of judgement or some such thing.'

Later, on the internal telephone, Nick Elliott and Dick White had, perforce, to confront the problem face-to-face.

The absolute rock bottom, they agreed, was that Sir Anthony Eden must not know the truth of what had happened. Not just Eden, but anyone of any influence who might pass it up the line. It was the biggest secret, and embarrassment, since the war.

That evening, though, the First Lord of the Admiralty found himself seated alongside one of the Soviets at dinner. A charming man, in naval uniform, who spoke English with hardly any accent, and thus was almost certainly a spy.

'My question is simple, sir,' he said. 'Why was there an English frogman swimming near our ships this morning? Please tell me it was an accident.'

Even at a State occasion there are ways and means. The First Lord treated the question as if it were a joke, and excused himself a mere two minutes later 'with a sudden call of nature.' When he returned he did not dissimulate.

'I have spoken to the Commander-in-Chief at Portsmouth, sir,' he said. 'It appears you have been misinformed. He has no record at all of any such activity. Could your informant, perhaps—?'

'Be mistaken? Blind? Blind drunk? We are, sir, Russians after all!'

The level of urbanity was impressive, and appreciated. But the Russian did not take his eyes off the First Lord's, and did not back down. The Englishman took a sip of claret, then cleared his throat.

'Very amusing, sir. I assure you that our sailors, also, like a drop or two of...well. Well sir, the point is I understand you are not speaking lightly, and my answer is a preliminary one. The C-in-C has had no reports so far – if he had, you would have been the first to know, I promise you. But that is by no means the end of it. Even as we sit here, wheels are in train.'

'Wheels? Trains?'

'There will be an immediate and full enquiry. He has had notice of trials of some equipment along the coast a little way – not actually in the harbour – and will get his people to go over everything with a fine tooth comb.' He smiled. 'Another Anglicism. I hope you understand.'

The Russian was as bald as a coot. He smiled.

'I have no need of such technology myself, sir. But I would like a quick report from Portsmouth. It is, naturally, a cause of some concern.'

More sips of claret. The First Lord then asked,

tentatively, 'Will there be a protest, sir? Before the matter has been looked into? I am positive there is a perfect explanation.'

They understood each other. 'And so am I, sir. So am I.'

Twenty Seven

Behind the scenes, however, as the banqueting went on, no one was certain what to understand. During his 'call of nature' the First Lord had met Ian Fleming, whom he imagined might have an explanation, and put the cat among the pigeons. Nick Elliott was informed, then went through his department like a dose of salts, kicking arse in plenty.

Although he did not show it, Elliott was a little drunk by this stage of the evening. While not invited to the banquet, he had had a session in the club with Philby and some others of the Barons, and their shared distaste for MI5 had called forth a fairly lethal mix of adrenaline and alcohol.

Back in the office, when Marion mentioned one name once too often, he blew his top. He was under pressure. It was getting worse and worse. And the pretty little poppet had become a nag.

'Pat Rose, Pat Rose, Pat fucking Rose, I'm sick to death of her!' he snapped. 'So she is worried, she's upset – and how the hell did she get through to us? Good heavens, Marion, there's a fucking war on!'

Marion's jaw was set. There was not a war on, but

there was a serious lack of sympathy. Or empathy. Or anything.

Pat Rose, she felt, must be looked after. She was suffering.

'Sir,' she said. 'I spoke to her myself. Sydney Knowles got her through to me. She's down in Portsmouth. She's been to the hotel. She's in a state. She's near collapse.'

His eyes were close to bulging. He could not believe his ears.

'You spoke to her?' he said. 'You *spoke* to her? On whose behalf, for God's sake? On whose *authority*? Good God, Miss Wilson this is a sacking matter. This is treason!'

Her face was pale. Her hands were trembling. She felt a great distaste.

'He said that he would ring her,' she said. 'Commander Crabb did. She stayed in a town just outside Portsmouth last night. Havant. With friends. Apparently a man called Pendock, Lionel Crabb's employer. They know all about it, sir. He said he'd ring her when it was over. They were getting married, sir.'

'Knowles,' he said. 'I'll have his guts for ribbons. That is treachery. I will have Knowles hanged for that. Who does he think he is, the turncoat? How *dare* he speak to that old slut?'

Marion Wilson's face was like a mask. And her

phone rang. It was Sir John Sinclair, the Head of SIS. He was abroad, a fact he hoped would save him from the coming hurricane.

She picked up the receiver and held it out to Elliott. He looked as if he might smash her face with it, but as she flinched he put it to his mouth and smiled urbanely; not for her benefit but the caller's.

'Sir John,' he said. 'How good to hear you! I promise you it's all in hand, sir, nothing to worry about. I've covered Portsmouth with the Official Secrets Act. Yes, all of it. Nothing in the world's a problem, sir. Nothing. And Buster Crabb is still alive, I promise you, he will turn up. Buster Crabb is still alive.'

He winked at Marion across the polished table. Marion thought she might be sick.

Twenty Eight

As far as Crabb could tell, the rifle bullets got him in the head. He heard them hit the water, two of them, a funny plopping noise, and he saw them as well, like snaky strings of bubbles just like worms. They bored down through the water in front of his visor, then turned back up towards the surface, did somersaults and drove down hard into his skull.

'Mum always says I'm thick,' he told himself, delightedly. 'Them bloody bullets would've killed a lesser man. Invincible!'

But he felt himself slipping downwards, down from the light surface to the darker depths. He reached out and took hold of a bilge-keel, or a bracket, and snagged his hand on something. Whoops, blood! That'll bring the sharks round. Whoops!

He looked around to see if he could spot Syd anywhere. Or indeed a shark. He felt down to his weighed belt and tried to feel the handle of his knife. No knife, no camera, no shark, no Syd. They'd had a lot of brushes with sharks out in the Med. A reason to wear gloves, in case you cut yourself. He'd once read that a shark could smell fresh blood a mile away. Silly that. My shark's got no nose. How does he smell? *Terrible*. Don't try to laugh though, Lionel. Dangerous. Oh. Lionel. Maybe time to come back to the surface. Oxygen Pete.

Down, down, down, down, down he slipped, watched by nothing more frightening than a gaggle of horse mackerel. They weren't frightening, he wasn't scared of them. They live on matelot shit, you know, can't get enough of it. If there were ten Navy ships in port, each with a thousand men say – how much shit was that? Ten thousand arseholes, was it? Bloody Ada. No wonder the fish were big as horses, the dirty bleeders.

Syd, where are you? Oh, you wouldn't come, would you? You said I was too old. It would've been a good earner, though, better than driving your bloody lorry. He wanted to laugh again, which was annoying. When would someone invent a mask that you could have a laugh in? Or a lorry, come to think of it, that didn't give you piles?

They'd come down to do the *Sverdlov* job last year in Syd's lorry, hadn't they? Or maybe he'd imagined it. OP did funny things to your brain, and talking of which, he'd just had two rifle slugs put in his skull. That was funny, too. They must've thought they'd killed him, but they hadn't.

British, he told himself! British to the core!

Dossveedarnya Russkie bullet! *Dossveefuckingdarnya!* That means goodbye. Hallo goodbye, you can't kill me, I'm British.

Knowles had picked him up in London last time after driving his lorry all the way from Blackburn, where he got his funny accent from. Long drive, but that was Syd. He'd given him forty quid to do the job, and all the diesel he could squeeze into his tank. Then he'd went and spoiled it all by not coming on the piss. It's a long drive back to Blackburn, Crabbie, he said. Yeah, and you're a fucking long time dead!

Good pal, though, Syd. Great skin. Great times they had out in the Med. First with the Davis escape gear, then they got the Eyetie frogman stuff. Fins instead of plimsolls on your feet! Lead weights on your belt instead of down your drawers, nestling against your wedding tackle! Happy days.

He didn't like the spy-men though, did he? He bloody hated Elliott and that gang, poofters who pretended they liked quim. Called Anthony Blunt the Queen Mother, but Bluntie's still in for a knighthood, in't he? He nearly got a bunch of fives from me, though, that time he thought I might bugger off to Russia. It's dangerous talk, that. People might get ideas. All sorts of them.

Out of the corner of his visor, Crabb caught a movement that made him jump. Bloody Ada, was that another frogman? Had Syd changed his mind and dashed down in his wagon from deepest Lancashire? Was it—

He realised he was close to the harbour bottom. The mud was gleaming at him through the murk, as though a hand-lamp beam had caught it. He gave some hard thrusts upwards with his fins, and crashed his shoulder into the cruiser's hull. Christ! Shit!

And he was weeping. Water squirting from his eyes, great gulps of oxygen going down his throat. Oh Pat, I didn't ring you, did I? Oh Pat, am I ever going to see you again? And what about that foursome? Poor Syd. He'll have to be best man. I will not take no for an answer. That's definite.

His head buzzed and sang. He was delirious. It's okay Syd, it's not much different to drinking whisky, is it, breathing oxygen? Another little drink.

Those dead Eyeties. Those wonderful brave blokes who only gave their gear up after they'd been killed by a depth charge blast, the pair of them. The tears squeezed faster, his vision down to five-eighths of fuck all. He wept for Margaret and the kids they'd never had. He thought of her and Pat Rose fighting over all the money he wouldn't leave, then damn near drowned of laughter.

You've always been a failure, Crabbie, even as a failure. A useless son, a useless husband, a useless seaman in the merchant navy. And then the diving, and the sudden joy. Vocation! You are a man, my son.

A *frog* man!

Oh God, what's that? Now that *is* a frogman! That's no mirage, that is someone on my shoulder! He's quick, he's agile and he's got a knife! He's got hold of my tubes! He's tearing at them, slashing, pulling, jerking. He's got a finger in my diving mask!

Oh, Christ, is this the dance of death? No, is it buggery! Away, away, away!

Twenty Nine

Syd Knowles found Pat Rose sitting on a bench outside Portsmouth Cathedral. She had been watching the door of the Sally Port Hotel and she was in tears. He touched her. She looked up and the tears became a storm of sobbing. He had a car these days, not a lorry, and he took her home to London in it.

'Don't try and ask them, Pat,' he said. 'I tried and I got threatened with the Secrets Act and worse. They're bastards, and what they're doing now is covering their backs. It's all they ever do. It's not us they're keeping safe, it's them. Just leave it, love. I'll stay down with you for a day or two if you've got no one else.'

'Is he dead?' said Pat. 'Sydney, tell me straight. Is Lionel dead?'

He could not tell her straight, because he did not know. It was most likely, but there was the other thing. He had gone to parties with Buster, and he'd been invited to more. The small man in the silly suit and hat, who twirled his swordstick like a picador – well, who knew? Was he mad, or a secret agent? The parties had been stuffed with young men, quite clearly homos, with people like Blunt and Burgess fawning over them. But Crabbie was no queer, he went through scrubbers like a dose of salts. He'd been the scourge of the Valetta dockside, famous for it. He'd been the man who put the horn in Leghorn.

'I guess he's dead, Pat, aye,' he said. 'Diving's a killing game, and Crabbie weren't fit, you know that, don't you? My guess would be a heart attack. That would be the quickest way.'

'You're kind,' said Pat. 'You're kind, Syd. You don't think he would have suffered, then?'

Syd shook his head.

'Not suffered, no. You know, love, underwater, when things go wrong...well, suddenly you feel right fine. You feel...comfortable. My guess would be that Crabbie's comfortable. Know what I mean?'

Maybe he's more comfortable than that, he thought. Maybe he's on the cruiser waiting to have drinks with Khrushchev and the other bugger when they get back from London. Maybe he'll be going off to Russia for a life of vodka and fat tarts.

He'd like that, probably. Good luck to him. Or maybe that goddamn Yank killed him, to stop that happening.

Nah, it would have been the fags and drink. Poor Crabbie was forty bleeding seven, with asthma and sugar diabetes for good luck. He bloody had it coming. With brass knobs on.

This was Nick Elliot's first and strongest line of argument as well, when it came to saving his position and the honour of the section. They managed to keep the disastrous operation from Eden for a remarkably long time, and when push came to shove, Elliott insisted that the whole thing had been authorised from above, he'd heard it personally from the FOA. What had killed Crabb, he insisted, was nothing more sinister than his lifestyle.

'There might conceivably have been equipment failure,' he said, 'but he almost certainly died of respiratory trouble, being a heavy smoker and not in the best of health. It's on record that he was urged not to undertake the operation, and he was indeed made to retire in 1955. His insistence was, he claimed, purely patriotic, because he loved his country. And I believe him. He was a hero, if a rather foolish one.'

Encouraged to say more, he put it this way: 'He begged me to let him on this mission, Prime Minister, he begged me on his bended knees. I begged him not to, with equal vehemence, but he was adamant. He was, indeed, a true-born British hero. English.'

Eden, in fact, had only got to hear that Crabb had disappeared a full ten days after the event. Navy Intelligence finally announced that he'd gone missing while doing test dives in Stokes Bay, three miles from Portsmouth Harbour, and although Elliott thought he was a milksop, Eden's reaction nearly blew the windows out. He was incandescent.

When he'd calmed down, he set on his attack dog, Norman Brook, to work out retribution. Eden admitted to a crowded Parliament that Crabb was tragically presumed to have lost his life in an accident, but added that the operation had been unauthorised. Ten days later he said that further, his own explicit orders had been disobeyed.

Nick Elliott, under appalling pressure, kept his London station out of it. He swore black was white that he believed people 'higher up' had cleared the operation, and when asked to explain the chain of command that had made the decision to overrule the Prime Minister, replied simply, 'We don't have one in SIS. We run more like a club.'

But while he escaped, his boss did not. Sir John Sinclair, although conveniently abroad when the 'horror' had occurred, was forced to retire by Sir Norman Brook – a mere grammar school boy – to be succeeded, as a final insult, by the boss of MI5, another scion of the middle classes. In the club that night, both Elliott and Philby wept into their metaphorical beer, although for different reasons. Damned Dick White had got control of their beloved service; the oiks had taken over. Just to rub it in, Brook had told the new man, with stunning indiscretion, that the PM was 'neither fit nor even rational.'

White himself did not want the move, because he wanted to consolidate his work at MI5 – including undermining Philby, whom he thought a traitor and Sinclair considered squeaky-clean, despite the evidence. However, Sir John at least managed to secure a knighthood for 'Queen Mum' Blunt, who was, indeed, the real Queen Mother's favourite, and could match her glass for glass of gin. They were soulmates; and, indeed, third cousins.

To the outside world, the switch was secret. It was unheard of for the head of the internal service to take on the foreign branch, so their natural antagonism went ballistic. The newspapers, dedicated to revealing such truths, however difficult, were unofficially advised to keep their pages empty of the subject. So they screwed their courage and their honour to the sticking post – and complied.

Nick Elliott, having successfully persuaded Sir Norman, later laid the blame on Eden anyway. The whole thing was a storm in a teacup, he said, and the PM had had a major tantrum because he hadn't been consulted.

Buster Crabb was laid to rest. Or would be, if they ever found a body. Ian Fleming didn't wait for that before he sketched out a thrilling novel. He would call it Thunderball.

Thirty

Pat Rose and Margaret Crabb had never agreed on much, nor did they tell the coroner the same thing when they went to identify the body found in Chichester harbour in June of 1957. Pat was 'pretty certain' it was not Lionel, Margaret thought it might well be.

Most other people had no idea at all. How could they, presented with an almost liquid corpse? It had been recovered leaking gouts of matter from the slits and orifices of a rubber frogman suit, with no hands or head, and writhing with a myriad of creeping, crawling sea-life.

Pat Rose, after she'd stared at it in horror, agreed with Syd Knowles that the missing parts were of significance.

'I mean,' she said, 'except for his nose and teeth, Lionel could have been anyone. Anyone small and little, anyway. I'd forgot how small he was, Syd. Poor little Crabbie. It could've been a little boy.'

'His hands,' said Syd. He remembered the occasions, and the waters they'd once dived in. 'They were tore to buggery. Steel wire. I'd've known them scars anywhere. Anyone who knew him would. Funny that the hands were gone as well.'

They left the morgue, left the other observers, and went to find a pub. After a year neither of them was too emotional, they'd got used to it. Except the fact that Syd had made him dive alone. Except the fact he'd disappeared so totally, for so very long. April to June. Fourteen months.

There was one other thing Syd Knowles thought, but he didn't say it to Pat because it might upset her; and anyway there was no way to be sure what it might mean. Whatever else the tides did, they didn't pull a dead man out of Pompey on the ebb, then squirt him up the next-but-one harbour entrance eastward down the coast to be conveniently found, however long it took. For two hours after high water Portsmouth, the Solent tide ran west not east, and a body, if it hadn't come up in half a week or so, would likely not come up at all. It was a fiddle. Stood to reason.

But the point of it? Syd didn't have a clue. Someone in the spook brigade had killed Crabbie, or he'd been whisked away to live a life of luxury by the Reds, what was the difference?

Or Crabb had choked to death on Grant's and poisoned oxygen, that was also possible.

Lots of other people did 'have a clue,' however. Some Labourites in Parliament even reckoned Earl Mountbatten had had a hand in it, but no one could come up with a convincing reason why. He was the First Sea Lord, not a Russian spy like 'Queen Mother' Blunt – though strangely, Marion discovered later, a woman called Kitty Jarvis knew Mountbatten, worked in the War Office, became Blunt's personal assistant – and was Crabb's unofficial 'aunt' as well. Which made her head hurt.

From the very off, the theories grew like mushrooms fed on bullshit. *Time* magazine suggested Crabb might have been 'bumped off' and his corpse disposed of when the Russians put to sea, or perhaps he'd been whisked alive to Moscow for 'debriefing'. Others claimed that he'd defected, or been shot by snipers, or been brainwashed, or had been planted by SIS to become a double agent. Inevitably there were reported sightings, there always are, and it was also said he trained up Russian frogmen to new heights of expertise. No one mentioned that he could hardly take a deep breath without a coughing fit. And hated vodka.

Marion's favourite 'lunatic' was the medium who swore black was white she'd seen Crabb being sucked up into a 'sort of tube' beneath a warship ('undoubtedly a Russian one – you can always tell'), then squirted out again far out in the Atlantic. Miss Wilson discussed it delightedly with her girlfriends.

'It's the sort of thing my Auntie Vickie says,' she told Charlotte. 'I think Pat Rose's Mr Pendock must have hired the clairvoyant for her name – Madame Theodosia! He paid her, too! There was another one, as well, perveying her barmy theories. They were like bees around a honey pot.'

'Wasps more like,' said Charlotte. 'People are horrible, aren't they?'

Pat herself, once she'd got used to it, grew philosophical. She went up to Blackburn for a holiday with Syd and Joan, and in the end they could have a sort of laugh about it.

'Whatever else,' she said, 'he was a kindly sort of bloke, and he had a sense of humour, that's for sure. I think he would have thought these theories were a load of...you know.'

'Conspiracies,' said Joan.

'Shite,' said Syd.

'It'd be nice though,' said Pat, 'if they had took him off to Russia, like. That's what

I'm going to believe, I reckon – even if it isn't true. He loved boiled spuds and big fat women. He always said I was a bit too thin for comfort. A bloody gentleman!'

Syd gave a final laugh.

'Whatever else, it were an accident,' he said. 'It stands to reason. There's not one of them halfwits in the spy brigade with brains enough to have worked it out on purpose. Poor old Crabbie drowned, I'd put good money on it.'

'Or had a heart attack,' said Pat. 'That's what I think. A quick clean, painless heart attack.'

'Aye,' said Joan Knowles. 'That would've been right nice for 'im; what he would've wanted.'

But Pat knew that she would not forget him, ever, and half believed he might one day turn up. His grave in Milton Cemetery, although strangely understated by orders of the Government, was rarely short of flowers, and his mother Daisy never ceased to insist he wasn't even in it. There was much talk of a mystery female admirer who tended the plot for years, and one of his relatives insisted, when DNA was discovered, that she would undergo a test, but never did. For Daisy, that seemed to prove her theory, somehow.

Peter Wright, of MI5, had he been asked, would have agreed with Syd. Wright thought the whole fiasco said everything one needed to know about MI6 – a bog-standard piece of gung-ho adventurism, badly conceived and worse executed. This brought a passionate riposte from the deputy director, George Kennedy Young, who defended Nick Elliott as a guardian of integrity in a 'world of increasing lawlessness, cruelty and corruption.' And later went on himself to try and found a private right-wing army.

The coroner, rather strangely, certified that the body was definitely Crabb, but returned an open verdict on the cause of death. The Government, with its usual insouciance, decided that all papers on the matter would be closed until 2057. Normally the term is thirty years.

No one believed Koltsov when he said years later that he had definitely cut Crabb's oxygen pipe as well as stabbing him to death, and sailors who claimed they had shot him in the head similarly failed to get their names in lights. Roll on 2057.

Thirty One

Oh Christ, thought Crabbie, beset by pain and shadows in the depths of Portsmouth Harbour, oh Christ, is this the dance of death? Those two men aren't real, are they? Or if they are, they've gone. The phantom frogmen. Oh Jesus, that's not funny.

He filled his lungs, and clenched his jaw, and struck out boldly upwards once again. Upwards and away.

I could kill a glass of Grant's, he thought. Come on, *tovarich*! I'm going to find your secrets now! And then a glass of Grant's.

Then they were back again. The shadows.

Oh God, what's that? That *is* a frogman! That's no mirage, that is someone on my shoulder! He's quick, he's agile, and he's got a knife! He's got hold of my tubes! He's tearing at them, slashing, pulling, jerking. He's got a finger in my diving mask!

Now two of them again! This *is* the dance of death!

And then it wasn't. No knife, a trick of light. And the frogmen had their arms out, they were coming to greet him, like a long-lost brother. They were gesturing. Upwards! Towards the surface. Towards a hatchway in the hull that he somehow hadn't noticed.

Suddenly it was crystal clear. Sydney had been right! They were going to take him back to Moscow, to become a hero of the Soviet Republic. He would spy for them, and teach them underwater warfare. He would be rich, and swan around with Burgess and Maclean.

Treachery? What the fuck was treachery? He came from Streatham, did little Lionel, his father's name was Hughie and his mother was a cook.

He hadn't gone to Eton, they'd sent him to a proper school, a proper English education. The posh boys were the traitors, the posh boys who didn't know the price of milk. He was Lionel Crabb, salt of the earth.

He would be welcome. The arms of Mother Russia. She would look after him. And Buster Crabb was drifting down again. Just drifting.

About the Author

Jan Needle has written more than 50 novels, as well as plays for stage, TV and radio, and several of his books have been televised. As well as thrillers, he writes highly acclaimed historical naval fiction, and has just finished the third of a series of novellas based around Nelson's life.

His first book, Wild Wood – an 'alternative view' of Kenneth Grahame's masterpiece Wind in the Willows – is recognized as a comedy spanning every age range in a newly revised edition which enhances William Rushton's superb illustrations. Toad is not the hero, but the original fatcat River Banker, spreading mayhem across the lush English countryside, and provoking a full-scale revolution among the local stoats, ferrets and weasels.

Jan lives in the North of England and has five children and six boats. He plays mandola, tin whistle, ukulele and accordion. Sadly, a pretty lousy singer though.

If you enjoyed *In Too Deep* you might like to try

Napoleon – The Escape

Napoleon – The Escape

Historical Note

"St. Helena! The very idea fills me with horror. To be relegated for life to an island within the tropics, at a vast distance from any continent, cut off from all communication with the world, and from all that it holds that is dear to my heart. That is worse than the iron cage of Tamerlane."

Napoleon, on the frigate Bellerophon, 1815.

The Emperor Napoleon was possibly the greatest general who ever lived – even the Duke of Wellington insisted on that – and it was imperative he should never roam free again after his defeat at Waterloo. His earlier escape from the Mediterranean isle of Elba had led directly to that battle, so now the British exiled him to a tiny Atlantic outcrop 1200 miles from the nearest land. There, the mighty Bonaparte could rot his life away.

Napoleon, however, like many a dictator before and since, was revered almost as a god. Before he even reached St Helena in 1815 his Royal Navy ship *Northumberland* was harried by a privateer, and rescue plots were being hatched in several countries. His brother Joseph, then living in America, pledged thirty million francs to set him free, and when *The Times* announced he had escaped, dancing was reported in the streets of London. The French Revolution had, after all, brought in a popular new use for lamp-posts – gibbets for hanged aristocrats.

Strangest of all, given England's official hatred for him, great men and patriots flocked to his cause. Lord Cochrane, the brilliant frigate captain known as the Sea Wolf (and model for Jack Aubrey in the O'Brian books) joined forces with the dictator of Peru to spring Napoleon to found a new Empire of South America, while innovators and men of science were keen to help as well. Robert Fulton, the American builder of the world's first working submarine, collaborated with an Irish smuggler called Tom Johnson, who aimed to pluck Napoleon from the island and spirit him away beneath the waves. The dictator, whose wife had point-blank refused to share his exile, would leave an unknown number of illegitimate children behind.

St Helena was a hotbed of treachery and intrigue.

One of Napoleon's island mistresses was the wife of the Marquis de Montholon, who had been appointed by France to look after him, while his personal physician, an Irishman called O'Meara, might very well have poisoned him with arsenic.

The governor, Sir Hudson Lowe, hated him so passionately he finally declined to meet or talk with him, and when he died, refused to mark the tomb – while insisting that the body in it was indeed the dead dictator's. Largely because of such intrigues, the truth of that assertion has never been confirmed beyond all doubt, although a corpse was later exhumed from it and moved to Paris.

When the grave next door, though – thought to contain the bones of Bonaparte's servant Jean-Baptiste Cipriani – was opened some years later, it was empty. And Cipriani was reputed to be Napoleon's double. Or even, possibly, his half-brother.

Chapter One

Samson Armstrong only overheard the plot to save Napoleon because he needed money. He was in the Trinco Tavern, fast by the Thames at Blackwall, secreted in a brick cleft built by his friend the landlord for the purposes of eavesdropping. It was halfway up a chimney, and it came damn near to killing him.

The first accent Armstrong tuned into from the babble down below was a French one, which in itself was enough to prick up his ears. The war was long over, certainly, but to say Johnny Crapaud was anything but hated in England's capital would have been a marvel and a calumny. The first full word he picked out was even stranger. It was *l'Empereur* followed by the name *Napoleon*.

Armstrong, like many Englishmen, had good reason to hate the strutting booby who had cost his land so dear. Employed as a captain by the East India Company, his livelihood had been destroyed not only by the longest war in memory, but by the peace that followed. With the Corsican exiled to St Helena had come the slump. In the London River, ships swung rotting round their buoys in droves.

Samson Armstrong was a resourceful man, not given to self-pity. When he had seen which way the wind was blowing, he had gathered together what money he had scrimped up in the good times, sold every bit and bob he owned, and made an offer for the vessel he commanded. The *Tamarind*, built in India of teak, would last a hundred years – worms broke their teeth on that noble wood. He and his wife Eliza, though, almost broke their hearts surviving.

Thus, from cruel necessity, came the smuggling, and other bendings of the law. He used the "priesthole" not for a fee, but on a sharing basis. The landlord also suffered from the mean ways of John Company – as the East India was called – and had tipped him off this gathering might yield pickings. John Company was immensely rich, and it kept its men immensely poor. In Blackwall it was immensely hated.

Once sold to Captain Armstrong, the *Tamarind* – a fast, lean brig, and armed with eighteen guns – was slandered by the company as a privateer or pirate to keep down her trading opportunities, and their lawyers tried to shift her off the Blackwall moorings; with no success so long as he could scrape his dues together. For crew he had men he could call upon when work was found – all of them quite happy to break heads.

The chimney nook was smoky and precarious, with a crackling wood fire in the hearth below, and the French words made Armstrong crane out so far he gulped down a bolt of smoke. Then, as he muffled his fit of choking, a raucous English voice cut through. It was a country voice, rough and angry.

'*L'Empereur?*' it shouted. 'There is no *empereur* no more! Your Bonaparte is England's now, stuck on a dungheap a thousand miles from shore, not on soft Elba guarded by a bunch of Latin lack-a-days! Mend your language, or this whole venture's off!'

A cacophony rose up through the smoke, full of passion, incomprehensible. Samson heard Scottish accents, Irish, French, and Welsh. A clear English voice cut through them all at last.

'For God's sake, gentlemen! For the sake of sanity! If this scheme is to even have a chance, belay your passions! There is dignity at stake! The world is waiting on us!'

The Frenchman's voice drove on again. It was cutting, thin with bitterness.

'This Irishman wants forty thousand pounds,' it said. 'Forty thousand, for a little ship we have not even seen. The man is mad. The man is Irish. They are a nation that lives on dreams.'

'They are not a nation,' said someone else. 'They are—'

'Good Christ, sir, shut your mouth! We cannot

descend to faction fighting! Draw in your horns! Please to use your brain!'

'Talking of which brain,' bore on the Frenchman, 'it is not even a proper ship for all it costs so much. He says it goes beneath the water! He says it will come up on St Helena entirely unseen. It seems to me this man's demented. And forty thousand pounds is—'

'—not yours to quibble over! It is already pledged, already gained, your share's a fleabite anyway. Pay it, and the greatest general in the world is free again – how much is that worth to you? A groat? A florin? Nothing? Your stupidity is—'

'And what do you know of underwater ships?' another voice demanded. This one was Irish, verging on fury. 'Tom Johnson is an honourable man. You, sir, from what I hear, are merely a... a... banker!'

In his alcove, Samson Armstrong was delighted. A full scale row, and – if Blackwall kept up its usual standards – blood mixed in the sawdust on the floor. He had been suffering since his livelihood had slipped away, vaguely bereft, and the thought of fighting filled him with a sudden joy. Could he get down to join it? He snorted with amusement. Only if he became a fall of soot...

Someone was talking in full-flown French now, too fast for Samson to follow easily, but claiming to be some sort of secret operator, an *assassin*. That, surely, in any language, was a murderer?

Then the calming English tones were in command once more and, strangely, rang familiar. He checked himself, concentrated to blot out the counter sounds. A cultured voice, voice of an officer. Could it be someone that he knew?

'My dear Ledru,' this voice said, 'Mr Johnson is not merely honourable, but a man Napoleon holds in personal regard. Surely, in your tower of fine secrets, you know he demonstrated such a craft to the Emperor on the River Seine in person? Or were you a mere dog's body in those days?'

This was insulting, but delivered so sweetly that the French spy came as close to laughing as he ever could.

'Indeed 'tis so,' he said. 'In a part of the river it is my pleasure to swim in whenever I am at home. The results were inconclusive, but His Excellency did express himself impressed. Though Johnson, as I understood it, stole the concept off an American. A certain *Monsieur* Fulton.'

'Did you say "stole" sir?' said the furious Irishman.

'A mistranslation,' soothed the English officer. 'Both men have since improved on their submarine designs, and have in fact collaborated. Speaking as an investor myself, in steam and other innovations, I consider they are at the leading edge. Their ideas will guide us to the future.'

'I'll drink to that!' put in another man.

This was a voice Armstrong had not heard before, but it was full of bonhomie. It was rich, and redolent of plums and brandy, and it calmed the others down.

'I'll drink to that,' it said again, 'and I'd like to drink to all of us embarking on this fine adventure. Remember, gentlemen, our purpose. To the Irishmen amongst us, and to many of us English, Napoleon was the embodiment of the future we all crave. He brought destruction to the ancient houses and the older kingdoms of the continent, he tamed the Pope, gave succour to the common man. He was brought low by the genius of England it is true – but by God, that genius should now be used to set him free!'

'English genius?' the Hibernian grumbled. 'Wellington is an Irishman, and that's who brought him low.'

'And Blücher was a Prussian, and many say the victory was to him,' said another voice. 'The truth is it was a mighty battle, and to reward the man who lost so narrowly by exile to a barren rock, is dishonour of the highest order. Whatever else, Napoleon Bonaparte deserves not this. His destiny might yet rise to even greater things.'

'Greater things? He is a monster! Some say—'

'Gentlemen, gentlemen, please.' It was the English voice that Armstrong thought he knew. 'Some say one thing, some say another, it was always in the nature of the man. But I abjure you, remember why we gathered here today. This Tom Johnson, be he great inventor or a hopeful rogue, has promised us a demonstration, that he can get Boney off his island against whatever odds. For God's sake let us wait and see what happens.'

'It will be marvellous,' said an Irish voice.

'Aye, marvellous like the time the Crapauds came to rescue you at Bantry Bay!' a Scotsman mocked. 'The year of the French, my hairy errse!'

'Nor will this new Paddy come to save us now!' another cried. 'I will wager anything you like! Where is he, that is the question? He promised us a grand spectacular, the thundering of guns, a—'

At which point there came a huge explosion, maybe outside the tavern but maybe not. A shock that dislodged stones and soot all round Samson Armstrong in his nook, and damn nearly set him on fire in a whoosh of sparks and flame that burst up from the hearth below.

He had had his fall of soot.

Chapter Two

Tom Johnson had chosen the time and day for his demonstration with great care. The reward of forty thousand pounds – riches beyond the dreams of avarice to a man who'd spent too much of his life in debtors' prisons – had already been received in part, and indeed been spent. The French spy Ledru, although a most unpleasant man, had impressed on him that money was no object, and had spoken the magic words 'a million' on more than one occasion. Now was the day of days. If this came off, and he and the submarine survived, the venture would be on.

'You see, Arthur,' he told his freezing crewman, 'I have the gift of the gab, as don't we all, we lucky sons of Erin? Call it the gab, call it the blarney, but I had to talk the hind legs off two donkeys to make this all happen. And let me tell you, Sunny Jim, it was the hardest job I ever done.'

Arthur Preece managed a small laugh, to show appreciation. He was cold, he was almost perished to the bone, and he didn't think he could hold out alive for much longer.

'Harder than that time we run the blockade to

Dun Laoghaire in a summer tempest? Christ, Tom, we lost five men that time, five good men and a dog. I had to swim two mile against the tide just to get me feet on ground.'

'Away with you, that was easy. You come out of it, didn't you? And didn't I buy you a pretty sweet colleen to make it up to you? Sure, you're always moaning Arthur. Hold your mouth and concentrate. Look there – that raggy schooner. That's our target. That's the one we'll blow.'

He extracted a great turnip of a watch from deep inside his tarry jacket and stared at it. The submarine – the Wee Hobgoblin – was lighted inside by shaded candles, and the compartment the two men sat in was open to the London air. Her uppermost deck floated almost flush with the surface, and they were protected from lapping waves by a cockpit coaming. Preece controlled her with a single oar, a revolving paddle of Johnson's own design which, all things considered, almost did the job. On the bigger craft they had constructed, there were steam engines, and up to eight men at oars that worked through piercings in the hull, made waterproof with soft leather grommets and pounds of tallow. Almost waterproof.

'High water just five minutes since,' said Johnson, stuffing the timepiece back again. 'We fix the torpedo with the lanyard, trip off the timing clockwork, then let the ebb shoot us down the river like a filly at the

Curragh of Kildare. 'Cause when it goes, it'll kill every human fish for bloody miles around. We do not want to be among them fish, Arthur!'

Two minutes later, the submarine nubbed up to the schooner. She was a derelict, a victim of the postwar slump, waiting to sink and die like so many other honest toilers. She had no watchmen on board – watchmen had been priced out long ago – so the job was easy, muttered Arthur – no need to submerge. He got short shrift.

'So you're after dying, is it? Jaysus, you *spalpeen*, have you got no brain at all? They'll be looking out for us, for all you know.'

'I think I'm going to die of cold whatever happens, and who will that do good to? If they're meeting at the Trinco, they'll be drinking on a night like this, not looking out. Maybe they'll stand us to a dram or six when the balloon goes up.'

'Get off with you again, you fool. And if they *are* keeping watch, and seen us floating up the river like we have done, where's the submarine in that? Where's the worth of forty thousand pound?'

'Seen us? This fog's like bloody curdled milk, how would they spot us in a month of Sundays? Sure they won't see us, Tommy, sure they won't!'

'And you believe in fairies, Arthur, so check all the leaky places then pull the bungs out till we go down a bit. Need not be far, a couple of feet will be enough for this time. But if they have been looking they'll expect us to go down, and so we will. Now, come below with me and take up position at the porthole. There she bubbles! And down we go...'

To be quite frank, neither man felt full of bursting confidence that the trick would go the proper way. Each time the submarine went under they had a tearing doubt if they would smell fresh air and see the sky again. Despite the brilliant American, Robert Fulton. Despite Johnson's own hopeful insistence that men had been sailing boats beneath the waters since the times of Ancient Greece. But they clambered down the hatchway and pinned and screwed it tight behind them, and watched the weedy hull of the dying schooner as it slid past the thick glass they were staring through.

'You did loop our bow-rope round her anchor warp? You did leave it slack enough to slide?'

'I did, Captain. But talking of slack – should we not be standing still? Why is the tide dragging so strong at us? Hell, Captain, are your calculations gone awry?'

There was a note of panic in his voice, which Johnston stamped on heavily.

'Damn you, coward! Just work to do your part! Manipulate the petard! Get that line around the anchor rope so I can spark the mechanism!'

It was a complex job, which required all their

skill, operating their arms from inside canvas tubes protruding into the murky Thames, manipulating their fingers through thinner cotton bags, waxed and oiled for the flexing. And all the time the glass steamed over with their breath, and they wondered if they'd have enough air left to breath when they had to do the hard work of pumping water out.

'If we'd brought the bigger one,' said Arthur Preece, 'we'd have had more men to row us out of this. We need more strength, Tom. Tom! I fear we cannot do this!'

'Shut up, you lily-liver! Shut up, you turd! My God, Preece, this is the last time! You are not worth seven shades of shit!'

Suddenly there was a click, and his voice changed. Tom, indeed, was very fond of Arthur, who was the best man he'd ever recruited for this dangerous trade. So what that he was frightened? Why should he not be, in fact? Not too deep down inside himself, Johnson was frightened, too. Maybe he'd go back to smuggling, after all. Though where, in that trade, would he find forty thousand for one jolly little beano?

They watched in satisfaction as the clockwork timer clicked into gear, confident it would strike sparks inside its waterproof compartment to ignite the fuse to set off the torpedo. A funny word, but a word Tom loved. Even though it had been Robert

Fulton's. Bloody American.

And then it changed. The current, moving faster than it should have been, snagged their light line on the big anchor warp somehow, dragging them sideways. Both men scrabbled in their unwieldy arm-tubes to clear it, but the weight of the vessel jammed it tight and tighter with the ebb. The *Wee Hobgoblin*, with a mind all of her own, began to roll to larboard, dipping alarmingly into the muddy murk.

'Christ!' yelled Johnson. 'Slip it free, can't you! I've set the clockwork off! If we don't get out of here we're conger bait. The petard's about to blow.'

'How long?' said Arthur. 'Tom, you said you'd set a short fuse for a good quick show. How long?'

They had five minutes, perhaps less by now, so Tom refrained from speaking. He dragged frantically at the line, cursing the stiffness of the cotton mittens encasing his fingers, cursing the lack of light, the lack of space, the rising tide of terror. What a way to go, blown up to smithereens or choked in tons of London's liquid shit. Oh Christ, a glass of small ale in the Trinco Tavern!

'We need a knife!' Preece shouted.

'To nick the canvas and drown us on the spot? Aye, champion! Pull! That way! Harder! Twist!'

'How long?' roared Arthur. 'I've been married not a full month yet! Oh Tommy, what have you done to me?'

But Johnson had been pumping, and suddenly the vessel lifted and the rope moved up the cable, and then slipped free. Through the smeared and muddy glass they saw the petard give a little twirl or twist and slide towards its planned position.

'Huzzah!' yelled Tom. 'Torpedo gone! We have two minutes left! Huzzah!'

Two minutes was not enough, but what to do? What else but seize the oar, and bless the ripping current, and trust in their dear lord? Within seconds the schooner hull had disappeared, the liquid blackness of the Blackwall Reach had swallowed them, and both men were at the pumps, moving like automata, moving like men of steam and steel.

'If we can break the surface,' Tom gritted, 'then maybe we are saved. If the blast should take us underwater, then we are dead.'

'I'm just three weeks a husband,' Arthur wailed. 'Captain, you have surely murdered me.'

'Oh cease your lamentations,' Johnson said. 'They will avail you nought. And in any way, she was no—'

At which the bomb went up, as did the *Wee Hobgoblin* submarine. She cleared the surface of the Thames, in fact. Flew above the water, as she had swum under it. As she crashed back to the surface, her hatch burst open and she sank.

It was a marvel. Ballads were written on the subject. It was a great phenomenon.

Chapter Three

After the explosion came the fire. Despite her dereliction, the schooner was a mass of makeshift fuel. She was used for storing spars and canvas, old warps and cables, drums of paint and linseed, even bags of gunpowder well past their best from damp. The torpedo blast cut through her rotten planking, and despite the inrush of the filthy Thames, found instant kindling aplenty. She went up like the flames of hell.

Before Samson Armstrong had tripped and stumbled clear out of the Trinco's taproom hearth, the conspirators had quit the tavern and emptied to the street. Ledru and the plum-voiced man were in the van, but half the scum of Blackwall seemed set to join the party, uninvited. From every alley, and from half the ships moored up along the quay, men streamed in every stage of drunkenness and half-undress. Some few whores also, delighted by the chance to ease the boredom of their trade. And maybe pick a careless pocket to the bargain.

The fire was enormous. Over the months she'd lain there, the schooner's sails – left furled to save the cost and trouble of removing them for storage – had worked loose and easy, plucked and buffeted by the raucous winds, as if in anticipation of a good strong spark to liven their existence. The flames ran up the rigging at alarming speed, found the canvas, wormed into the folds and flappings, then burst into an orgy. The flames melted the pitch and broke off shorter lengths of burning cordage, which dropped onto the waiting lumber on the decks. To the watchers on the shore it was glorious.

'It will spread!' said Ledru. 'My good God, what a demonstration indeed! And nobody saw a thing! This boat that goes invisible is—'

For Ledru, Napoleon Bonaparte's most trusted personal assassin, this was an unusual piece of indiscretion. It was compounded when one of the other conspirators, pushing past the plum-voiced man, responded even more loudly – and entirely in French. What he said was not the question. Even in the lowest of the docks people knew the accent, and that accent screamed out *spy*.

Ledru had the finest instincts of a killer. He shot a glance of fury at the loose-mouthed underling, then, as people moved in on both of them, pointed at him, his face contorted, and shouted – in a nearly perfect copy of an English accent – 'He is a traitor! This man is French! He has set the ship ablaze!'

'*Non!*' screamed the man. '*Mais—*'

He saw Ledru's knife because he knew his man. Before the great assassin could notch another kill, his assistant had thrown himself sideways into the crowd which – being English possibly – parted momentarily. It was a moment though, no more. As the man began to run, hands seized at him, blows were aimed. Confusion saved him in the first seconds, but as he rushed across the quay he had a crowd of followers, a growing, baying crowd.

'He's French! He's French! They're burning London down!'

Unfortunately for him, it was at this moment that Captain Armstrong emerged into the outside world. Dark though it was inside the Trinco Tavern, the light outside was more dangerous yet for him, because the quay was lighted by the flickering, flaring extravagance from Tom Johnson's demonstration. And Samson looked just like an imp from hell.

'There's another one!' the cry went up. 'By Holy Christ and this one is a neger! He'll kill us all! He'll murder us!'

'No!' shouted Samson Armstrong. 'Friends, I am a Londoner! My ship is—'

A neger? he thought. My God, what is this? They cannot think that I am black!

But in a brighter flare he was enlightened. He had come down the blasted chimney like a climbing boy who had not washed for half a year. His clothes were filth, his hands and face were ebony, his eyes were no doubt glaring in their sockets, crying to be gouged out. Samson was not a fool. He did not stay to open a dispute.

All round him as he ran, the crowd was thickening and the noise was growing. From over on the waterside he heard reports that could be gunshots, and then another mighty whoosh as a second ship went up. It had been moored alongside the schooner, another derelict. There were clanging bells all round him now, and people shouting to rouse out the watch. But many men had time to try and bring him down and kill him. Armstrong, who could swim, charged forward with his shoulder, roared a battle cry, and dived into the icy river.

Oh you bastard, he thought, as the cold clenched his chest and made him gulp down air and water mixed. Oh you bastard. But I wonder if cold Father Thames will make me white again! And I wonder where the nearest steps might be!

When his head broke the surface, Samson found the river busy with new craft. Two navy cutters had rushed in, packed with marines with muskets and long pistols, and they were shooting every little thing that moved.

Soldiers, he thought. Soldiers are mad! They can't see what they're aiming at!

He had no idea himself, but he knew it must not

be him, in any circumstance. At which a buzzing ball sang past his head and smack into the stone quay wall. As he ducked he almost felt another one part his hair. He had a vision of Eliza, lying in their bed. Oh Christ, she did not even know where he had gone. Christ, when will we meet again?

The realization of how he'd left her fired him anew. She was all alone not far down the wharf on board the *Tamarind*, and God knew, the noise and rioting must surely have awoken her. She would be frantic, she'd be bereft, he had not even left her with a pistol for protection. If these men from Bedlam spread along the shore in rape and pillaging, what they would do to her?

By now his nose alone pierced through the surface, and his whole frame was rattling with the cold. No more shots came at him, but the jetty stones beside his face were thick with foetid slime. The noises were not hopeful, either. Screams and cries of agony, whoops of hunting as the mad dogs had their fun. This part of Blackwall was dangerous for the watch at dead of night in normal times. *This* dead of night was abnormal in extreme…

But he had to go. His lungs and muscles were beginning the start of seizure, his hands too numb to even feel the water they were moving in. He let the ebb tide take him along the wall, checking himself at every fissure and obstruction in case it was a ladder or a step. Christ, it was cold. Oh Christ, oh Christ, oh Christ. So cold.

And not three hundred yards away, a hasty shawl draped across her shoulders, Eliza Armstrong came on the deck of *Tamarind* to look for him. She had a lantern in her hand, which was a bad mistake. It threw no very useful light for her, but to any watchers she was revealed. Among the thick mist and the milling crowd, a big man stopped and looked, then moved towards the rail. The roar of fire from the schooner, the stench of smoke, clogged and blocked her lungs and choked her scream. Oh Samson. Oh my husband...

She ran back towards the cabin as he climbed on board. A big man, very big. And in his hand he had a pistol, which was also big, with double barrels.

Helpless, she tore at the cabin door latch. She was quite helpless.

*

Like Samson Armstrong, the spy Ledru's spurned helper was another strong and healthy man; and it saved him for a while.

By dint of force and courage he broke from the first pack that tried to kill him, and went into the alleys behind the quayside like a hunted hare. He moved in circles, too, just like a hare, because he hoped to confuse them. A man in his position should have run like an arrow, fast and straight, until the half-starved London ruffians had tired themselves to death. He knew these people. They had had no revolution, no Napoleon, they lived on scraps and shit, detritus from the rich man's groaning table.

But he also knew his London, or rather, he did not. He knew that this place, like every land of docks, was a warren inhabited by human rats, unmapped, unfathomable except by long usage and the ratlike instinct. If he ran in a straight line there would come a time that he was lost, a white rat in a land of black, a fat rat in a land of thin. Then they would fall on him, and kill him. They would eat up all the fat and leave the tail and gristle. Lucien Gauthier – such was his name – ran in a circle, like a hare.

He saw sights and sounds he hadn't seen since Robespierre's Great Terror. Corpses in the streets, part-dismembered or still alive to be gnawed at by the dogs, young women leaning against walls, semi-naked and wholly lost to reason, babies sucking gin from bottles, discarded beside their mothers grubby breasts. If Lucien had had a heart it would have broken. But Lucien, like his master Ledru, did not have a heart.

He came back to the chief *assassin* after half an hour, and although he was panting, he had shaken off his last pursuer. He came down a long alley back towards the Trinco quayside, and noted that the flames from off the water were dying down. There were still throngs, but they had thinned, and the gunshots had died away. His master, inevitably, like a wraith from out the sepulchre, was waiting for him where the alley opened out. Unlike Lucien, his breaths came normally. No signs of fear or effort.

'*Monsieur*,' said Lucien. 'You waited.'

Ledru moved towards him with a smile.

'And you,' he said, 'still speak in French. Will you never learn, *espèce de con*?'

And he slipped a long, sharp blade into the heaving stomach, twisted it, withdrew, and pushed his ex-assistant to the gutter to lie and die.

'Give me lucky men,' he muttered. It was, of course, a quote of his dear emperor. Well, almost.

In the water, Samson Armstrong had at long last found a ladder. He prayed to God he had the strength to use it. He was so cold; so cold.

Chapter Four

It was not cold on St Helena despite the height at which the two men stood, and in any case, Napoleon refused to feel such things. He had lost perhaps a hundred and fifty thousand men marching back from Moscow, betrayed by nothing but the snow and bad intelligence, but he had—

No, that was not all of the truth. Napoleon hated losing, but he valued honesty, when possible. The winter had been bad, his intelligence had been worse, but the Russians' tactics had been what mastered him. He turned away from gazing at the rolling South Atlantic and back to Montholon, who was actually shivering.

'You are a milksop, sir. When I marched back from Moscow my soldiers killed their horses and used them as warm overcoats, but I did not, over a thousand miles. I've a mind to order you to take yours off.'

Montholon said daringly, 'But it was hardly marching, was it? You rode a dozen horses quite to death, and sometimes took a carriage.'

'You are but a marquis, sir, I am an Emperor.

You would not have me walking like a common soldier, surely? And I only went on wheels when I was sleeping, to rebuild drained strength. If I had not rode I would have starved to death. True or false?'

It was true, and because of the tactic he so admired in his enemy. As the Russians had retreated east at first, before his *Grande Armée*, they had laid waste to every crop and berry, slaughtered every beast. And poisoned all the wells, to boot. And filled each pond and stream with rotting corpses, animal and human.

'You did everything you had to, Your Excellency, of that there is no doubt. One day, God willing, you will wreak your vengeance on the Russian Bear. Only you can do it.'

It was the right answer, in the right tone of voice. Montholon did not believe it any longer, and frankly did not care. Napoleon had done him harm enough, both before and after bringing him to this island as his aide, and done it quite devoid of ruth. Montholon suspected, but did not know, that he had made him a cuckold, also. If his wife's expected baby came cooing Corsican, he told himself morosely, he would be sure. Much good that it would do him.

'Near two thousand feet above the sea up here,' said Napoleon, reflectively. 'The wild Atlantic that every man's afraid of, except for English sailors, they would claim, damn them. Ha! And it's not even cold.

I wonder what it's like in London, Montholon. You know the date, don't you?'

It was burned on both their minds. It was the date the Irish smuggler Tom Johnson had undertook to set the thing in motion, to suit the tides and phases of the moon. Hard to believe that over there in England it would be as cold as charity, with violent gales perhaps.

'Indeed I do, Excellency. But forgive me if I do not share your confidence that it will happen as to plan. Johnson is Irish, after all.'

'And a smuggler since twelve years old. He has made and lost some fortunes, and do not tell me it's romance, Charles Tristan, for I met the man in Paris, along with Fulton the American, and saw their *bateau invisible* in action. Fulton has made such craft for many people, and Pitt himself has given him money for research. Great stores of money. A hundred thousand *livres* I have heard.'

Talking with Napoleon, like with any great dictator, was a game of skill. Montholon had his own ideas about the value of these secret weapon stories, and he knew exactly when to argue. Not now. He smiled and pointed.

'Look, Excellency. See there. A ship, a big one, coming up from the Cape, I suppose. Who knows, she might have your submarines on board!'

Napoleon said irascibly, 'Even that skinny little

bastard Nelson could not have made a ship arrive that fast. Whore-monger.'

'Indeed, my lord. But surely it will not be very long, will it? If Captain Johnson has proved his worth today, Ledru will pay him the balance of our money and the other interested parties will do the same. Good God, sir, the weapons could be at sea tomorrow! And then how long? Six weeks? Two months? Communications are miraculously improved these days.'

'You're in the land of fantasy, Charles Tristan, but it is a pleasant realm. And we've been at this escape so long that something will go right one day, I'll bet your life on it.'

Thank you indeed, thought Montholon. *Your grace amazes me.*

There had indeed been much energy expended since Napoleon had landed at James Town the October after Waterloo, and many pounds and many francs had been disbursed. An American privateer called the *True Blooded Yankee* had been set on by revolutionists in Buenos Aires to harry the English before the prisoner had even reached the island, and the Emperor's brother Joseph still pledged solemnly he would spend his fortune to set him free. To many, Bonaparte was the only hope to finish urgent business.

Racked with misery and boredom on this ocean

pimple, the Corsican himself clung to the dreams through thick and thin, egged on by many men for many reasons. Spies and mountebanks smuggled ideas and plans ashore, and the schemes they brought were legion. Steam vessels were suggested, tall Yankee ships with more canvas than a snow-clad mountain, even air balloons. The English responded with naval bases set up at Tristan da Cunha and Ascension Island, so far into the wastes of water that most considered them a jest.

The governor of the island, a hard-faced Englishman called Sir Hudson Lowe, seemed to understand Napoleon's most desperate needs with uncanny prescience. His cordon of security was so oppressive that even the guards were sometimes flogged for the *major sin* of not flying the right-coloured bunting if the prisoner strayed outside a zone. Every part of the island had its code flag, that had to be run up when he entered it or left. When dark had fallen he could not move at all.

On top of this, a system of semaphores relayed the Corsican's precise whereabouts at any time, which probably meant the governor could have told the Marquis de Montholon the exact time and date his wife had received the alien seed. Certainly he had known when another bastard had been planted in the virgin English womb of Lucia Balcombe, who had been banished from the island with her parents by Sir

Hudson, on the grounds that she might be a spy – or, if it came to term, give birth to one.

High on the peak of Mount Diana, as the sun dropped into the western sea, Montholon shivered yet again, and even Napoleon allowed the rising breeze to be a shade uncomfortable.

'In any case,' he said, 'that ship is not bringing our saviour *sous marin*, nor must we fall into the sin of unsoldierly impatience. I have a feeling, Charles Tristan, that our Irish rogue has done the deed, and the man they call the Sea Wolf will have aided him. The Sea Wolf is a formidable man.'

'Indeed,' breathed Montholon. He shivered once more, and violently, with relief at deliverance from the mountain wind. 'Lord Cochrane is by far a greater sailor than Horatio, by any measure. And he is our friend.'

The two men moved towards the downward track. A half a mile away a signal flag was lowered.